"You don't think this was a hunting accident?"

I glanced around. The church was in an isolated location, a no-hunting zone, next to the woods. It was hunting season. "Maybe. I guess it could have been." But even as I said the words, I didn't believe them. Something inside me was tingling. I wasn't sure why, but my gut told me this wasn't an accident.

Other mysteries by Candice Speare

Murder in the Milk Case
Band Room Bash

Don't miss out on any of our great mysteries. Contact us at the following address for information on our newest releases and club information:

Heartsong Presents—MYSTERIES! Readers' Service
PO Box 721
Uhrichsville, OH 44683
Web site: www.heartsongmysteries.com

Or for faster action, call 1-740-922-7280.

Kitty Litter Killer

A Trish Cunningham Mystery

Candice Speare

HEARTSONG
PRESENTS
MYSTERIES

Acknowledgments:

An author doesn't write a book alone, despite the long hours of isolated pecking at the computer keyboard. I will never be able to express enough gratitude to the following people: Susan Downs, my editor and friend; Joyce Gray, whose humor helps me find my sanity when I lose it; Thelma Mills, my mom and a brainstorming powerhouse; Brad Speare, who has always believed in my dream; Elizabeth Grosskopf, Diana Blessing, and Bryon Miller, who are always there for me; Nancy Toback, an expert at finding the things I overlook; Ellen Tarver, my favorite line editor. Finally, special thanks to Lt. Glenn Rambo with RS Writing Services. His expert and generous input gave much-needed authenticity to my law enforcement scenes. (If there are mistakes in this book, be they police procedural or anything else, I take full responsibility. It simply means I wasn't paying close enough attention to what people told me.)

© 2008 by Candice Speare.

ISBN 978-1-60260-071-3

Cover design: Kirk DouPonce, DogEared Design
Cover illustration: Jody Williams

Our mission is to publish and distribute inspirational products offering exceptional value and biblical encouragement to the masses.

Printed in the U.S.A.

1

I've often thought it interesting how an emotion like love—or the perception of love—can make a person act irrationally and do things totally out of character.

Take this morning, for instance. I was sitting in my SUV, Monday midmorning, in the throes of lethargic indecision, parked in front of Adler's Pet Emporium. Chris, my thirteen-month-old son, was throwing a tantrum in his car seat. I dug my nails into my palms to keep myself from banging my head on the steering wheel with the rhythm of his pounding heels. Not because I was frustrated with him. Temper tantrums were his regular mode of communication lately, so I just tried to ignore them.

No, I had to make a decision. Did I want to be selfish, break my daughter Sammie's heart, and tell her she couldn't have the pedigreed Siamese kitten my mother-in-law had purchased for her? Or would I put up with a house cat because I loved my daughter enough to sacrifice for her? Not to mention adoring my husband, Max, enough to allow his mother to do something like this to me without first asking my permission.

Head banging would momentarily distract me from my dilemma, but despite feeling lethargic, I could no longer avoid making the decision. As my mother would say, "Never put off until tomorrow what you can do today."

I bit a nail and considered the possibilities. The kitten was still at the breeder's. That meant I had time for a desperate act—like coming down with a sudden, raging cat allergy that would kill me if I inhaled enough cat dander. Of course, that would be a lie. And true love doesn't lie.

I turned to look at Chris, whose face was tomato red. "Just hang on, grumpy."

I buttoned my coat against the brisk November cold, got out of the car, and opened the door to the backseat. Chris immediately stopped crying, reached out his arms, and beamed at me. Let anyone tell me that babies aren't born manipulators! I kissed both his cheeks. Then I snugged a hat over his head, zippered his little blue coat, and hefted him from the car.

The pet store occupied one end of a small strip mall in Four Oaks. My mother's doughnut shop occupied the other end. In between were little stores that changed owners on a regular basis because our rural location can't sustain the business. Especially with the advent of megastores that offer impossibly low prices on everything.

I sneezed when I entered Adler's Pet Emporium, an ambitious name for the family-owned business that consisted of only two stores. Maybe I really was allergic.

"Trish Cunningham. What a nice surprise on a Monday morning. You just bring that baby right over here to me. Your mother talks about him all the time." Jaylene Adler reached out for my son from behind the counter. Her big black beehive hair didn't move. She'd had the same hairstyle for as long as I could remember.

I gladly obeyed. She took Chris from my arms, and he smiled broadly, the little charmer. He happily let her remove his hat and coat.

"I do so wish I had more grandbabies. My oldest is almost nine. Peggy's daughter? She's coming into town to visit me for a week while her mama goes on a business trip with her husband."

I remembered Peggy. During high school, she'd attended a private boarding school in Michigan. That's where she lived with her husband. I hadn't seen them in a long time. "How is she doing?"

"Great. Really great. Her husband is really moving up in the world." She tickled Chris's tummy, and he giggled. "So what are you here for?" she asked between coochie-coos.

"Stuff for a new cat. My mother-in-law thought Sammie needed a pet now that she has a new little brother. We're picking up the cat in the next couple of weeks. Siamese."

"You getting it from that breeder out there near Brownsville?" Jaylene asked.

"Yes. Some friend of my mother-in-law's. Hayley, I think her name is?"

"I order all her supplies," Jaylene said. "Now. . .you'll need the works." She nodded toward the back of the store. "Row four, back right corner. You go on while I hold little Chris here, and I'll get my lazy bum of a husband to help you." She turned around. "Hen-*ry*? Little Trish Cunningham is here and needs help."

I found it amusing that I was still Little Trish Cunningham to her. She and Henry had been friends of my family for as long as I could remember.

I wandered to the back of the store, past the dog aisle, and sighed as I glimpsed a sturdy leather collar and leash. A dog would be so much better than a cat. Maybe a border collie like my father's dog, Buddy. Dogs were just so much less elusive and sneaky than cats.

In the back of the store, I picked up a small bag of cat litter, felt something hit my feet, and looked down to see a tiny stream of litter flowing from a hole in the bag.

Henry appeared as I tried in vain to stop the litter dribbling onto my feet and into my shoes.

"Trish, good to see you. I'm lookin' forward to seein' your daddy soon to do a little huntin'."

"He's looking forward to it, too. Keeps us all stocked up in venison." I pointed to the floor. "Um, there's a bit of a mess here. This has a hole in it." His gaze fell on the bag then on the trail of kitty litter that had fallen to the floor. He mumbled something that sounded suspiciously like a swear word as he reached out with meaty hands and took the leaking bag from my arms.

"Jaylene!" he yelled. "We got a mess back here."

I heard her footsteps as she strode to the back of the store, still holding Chris.

"What's wrong that you can't handle?" she asked.

He pointed at the floor. "A hole in the kitty litter."

"Well then, clean it up," she snapped and whirled away. "The dustpan's in the back. I can't help it. It's 'cause of that new WWPS delivery guy. He punched holes in two other bags, too." She marched past a fish tank display. "I'll call the WWPS place and complain."

"Thanks for nothing," he grumbled as he glared at her back.

"And while you're at it," she said from two aisles over, "you need to pack those boxes that have to go out before he gets here."

Jaylene and Henry were getting along as usual, which meant they weren't. Sometimes I find comfort in knowing that some things never change; however, marital discord isn't on my favorites list.

Henry's paunch jiggled as he put the leaky bag aside and picked up a larger one for me. "You'll need more than that."

"Why? It's only a small kitten," I said.

"You'll want to scoop the litter twice a day. Keep the kids from playing in it."

That was a thought that hadn't occurred to me, and I didn't like the picture I got in my head. Maybe a cat wasn't such a good idea after all. But I wouldn't change my mind now.

"I also need a crate," I said.

"Well, you're in luck. We have those in stock here. Won't have to get it from the other store."

I made my choices, and Henry followed me, carrying the heavier items to the counter for me, where Chris burbled happily in Jaylene's arms.

"I'll get that crate," Henry said as he went into the back room.

"While he gets that, you need to pick out a kitty collar." Jaylene pointed to a rack of custom-made collars next to the counter. "This is my specialty, you know. I make these and sell them over the Internet. I also carry a line of pet toys and clothes."

"I know," I said. "I saw your display at the festival last Saturday." Everyone with any kind of business had a booth at the Four Oaks Fall Festival each year.

I stared at the collars, thinking how much the kitten was going to hate wearing one, but to save my time and energy, I didn't argue. I snatched a blue one from the rack.

"So I hear from your mother that Abbie Grenville is getting married," Jaylene said. "To that police detective."

I nodded. My best friend's wedding was in two weeks and six days.

Jaylene handed Chris back to me as she began to ring up my purchases. "What's the detective's name? Scotch?"

"Scott," I said. "Eric Scott."

"Not a local boy, is he?"

"No," I said.

"Well, not like her first husband, which is a good thing. You know that Philip's mama still lives near here." She took a breath. "That Scott fellow. . .he was the one you helped solve that teacher's killing over there at the high school last year, right?"

Obviously Jaylene had been talking to my mother, who is convinced that the cops can't figure out a murder without me. "*He* solved that murder. Not me."

"Well, that's not how your mama tells it," Jaylene said.

"It's not true." I spend way too much time denying the rumors my mother spreads about me—good and bad.

"Anyway," Jaylene continued, "being married to a cop will certainly be handy for Abbie's books. All that scary stuff she writes. I bought a copy of her latest book when she did that book signing thing at the festival, but I'm not going to read it."

I didn't think the books Abbie wrote were *that* scary, just typical suspense.

Jaylene glanced over her shoulder then leaned toward me. "Besides, it might give me ideas." She said the words in a stage whisper.

I winced. "Ideas?"

"You know what her book is about. Killing *somebody* off." She nodded at the door where Henry had disappeared. "Sometimes husbands just get on your nerves."

Abbie would be troubled to know that her book might inspire someone to kill. If only Jaylene would say something nice to Henry and ease the tension in the room.

He wandered out of the back room and came up behind Jaylene. I balanced Chris on my hip.

Jaylene frowned at Henry when he started to paw through papers and receipts in a drawer under the cash register. Several fell to the floor as his search grew more intense. "You seen that receipt for my new rifle?" he asked. "I gotta go back to the gun shop and get somethin' fixed. Goin' huntin' this weekend."

"You got that gun?" Jaylene turned on him as though she were going to hit him.

Henry glanced at me then back at her. "We'll discuss it later."

"You better believe we will. And the stuff in this drawer is just pet store stuff. Why would it be here?"

" 'Cause I put it here." He kept digging.

Jaylene's breath hissed through her teeth, and she turned her back on him. I could see her trying to pull herself together. "Your mama said she's doing the catering for the reception even though she's been out of the catering business for a while."

My mother's shop, Doris's Doughnuts, is gossip central. I was sure everyone knew everything about the wedding since it was one of my mother's favorite latest topics.

"Yep." I glanced at my watch. "In fact, I've got to get going. I promised her I'd stop by so she could see Chris."

Jaylene glanced at Henry. "Take this stuff to Trish's car."

Since Henry was already piling my purchases in his arms, I thought maybe her orders were unnecessary. "Gimme your keys," he growled at me.

I did, and he walked away mumbling. I set Chris on the counter for a moment while I fumbled my wallet out of my purse and started counting out money.

"Weird, Abbie gettin' married, and her ex-husband shows up all the way from New York City," Jaylene murmured as she watched me.

"What?" I glanced up, dropping a five-dollar bill on the floor. Then Chris shoved my purse. It fell over, and though the contents spilled all over the counter and onto the floor at Jaylene's feet, I was too startled by her words to pay much attention. "Philip is in town?"

"Yes." The word sounded harsh as she bent to pick up my belongings.

"Have you seen him?" I asked as I began to stuff things back into my bag.

Jaylene stood up and handed me my cell phone, some tissues, and a small pile of receipts. "Henry saw him. Haven't seen him myself. He's a pitiful excuse for a man."

In a way, that was a true statement. Philip had never been faithful to Abbie, which is why their marriage ended. I wondered if Abbie knew he was in town.

From the corner of my eye, I saw Henry loading my stuff in my SUV. Chris was bouncing on my hip and kicking my thigh.

Jaylene followed my gaze and then rolled her eyes. "He says I'm a tyrant, but if I don't ride him, he'd get nothin' done all day." She took my cash from my hand,

and I leaned over to pick up the five-dollar bill. I still had kitty litter on my shoes. I stood up again, and Jaylene slapped my change on the counter. Then she stretched over and rubbed Chris's head. "Bring him back in to see me again."

"Will do," I said. I tucked Chris into his coat, then I slung my purse over one shoulder and my son over the other. Henry handed me my keys on my way out the door.

"You take care now," he said.

"You, too," I murmured.

I could barely think. I was stunned that Philip was back in town. I needed to find out more, and I knew just the place to start. I left my SUV parked where it was and ambled down the sidewalk to Doris's Doughnuts. I was under strict orders to bring Chris by to visit my mother whenever I was running errands. I dared not disobey her. She always seemed to know when I was out and about. A stranger might think she had some sort of supernatural GPS system to keep track of me, but I knew better. She had informants. Besides, today my vehicle was parked within her sight. I had no choice.

As I walked, I speculated about how small my world had become since the birth of my fifth child. Well, technically my second, but I viewed my stepchildren as my very own.

I used to work part-time for our family self-storage business, one of Max's family's ventures. But I'd taken time off after Chris was born, and now the biggest event of my day was buying supplies for a new cat and visiting my mother's shop.

Unlike many women who adore being home all the

time, I missed working.

I opened the glass front door of Doris's Doughnuts, and a bell announced my entrance. A blast of cold air blew past me, tangling my already messy hair and riffling the papers hanging on a bulletin board on the wall.

The cheery red and white dining area was almost half full, even at midmorning. Ma's shop was *the* place in town to get a good cup of coffee. It rivaled that of any specialty coffee chain. She'd started out in the catering business, and then she'd opened the shop. Once it began to take off, she stopped catering on a regular basis. And a few years ago, she'd expanded the shop hours, adding lunch sandwiches and other baked goods.

Chris was wiggling in my arms as I walked toward the glass-enclosed counter.

"Well, look who the wind blew in," Gail, my mother's right-hand gal, said. "Doris didn't say she was expecting you. Then again, she doesn't tell me much these days."

"You know everything you need to know," Ma growled at Gail while she snatched Chris from me. "You come right here to your granny."

I let him go and looked at the two women in surprise. They rarely fought. When they did, it was the proverbial battle of the titans and rarely lasted more than a few hours, which was a good thing. The force of their joint anger had the potential to destroy half the town.

"I'm glad your mommy finally decided to come by and visit Grandma," Ma said to Chris, who grinned at her. "Your auntie Abbie has been here for two days straight."

I blew out an exasperated breath. "Of course she's been here, Ma. You're catering her reception. She needs to talk to you about it. Besides, I was here two days ago."

I don't know why I bothered defending myself. It was a lost cause. I dismissed her manipulation and perused the menu.

"We're selling Abbie's latest book." Ma pointed at the counter near the cash register. "She came by with some copies. April May set up a display this morning."

I'd missed it due to my son's squirming, but I looked now, and I was impressed. April had done a good job. The black book cover with the profiles of a man and a woman, with the graphic of a sparkling gray bullet superimposed between them, was simple but attention-grabbing. This book was Abbie's best suspense yet and her first to win real accolades. It read like a true story about a man who plans his ex-wife's murder and almost gets away with it.

"She's going to be a celebrity bride," Ma said. "We might have to keep the paparazzi away from the church during her wedding."

"I doubt that." I grinned at her flair for the dramatic.

"Your mother just wants the publicity so she can expand and leave her friends behind," Gail snarled as she sideswiped my mother on her way to make a shot of espresso for a customer.

Ma glared after her then turned back to me, jiggling Chris on her hip. "Are you and Max still thinking about buying a new house?"

"Maybe—why?" I couldn't decide what to eat.

"Linda Faye King has her real estate license now. And she's working for me part-time in the mornings."

Gail snorted and slammed a ceramic mug on the counter. I blinked, surprised it didn't crack.

Ma rolled her eyes.

"So Linda's not working in the hospital emergency room anymore?" I asked.

"No."

"She says she quit, but. . ." Gail's words trailed off, leaving no doubt that she was suspicious of Linda's exit from her job.

"Linda just got tired of the hospital," Ma snapped. "I told her you and Max need to move, so she's looking for houses for you."

"I didn't say it was a for-sure thing." Had my confidence level so diminished since I'd stopped working that I was letting everyone boss me around?

"You know what they say," Ma intoned. "The early bird gets the worm. You can never be too prepared." My mother has an encyclopedia of platitudes embedded in her brain.

Gail snorted louder and stomped to the back room. I wondered what was up with the two of them. I also realized I wasn't going to be able to stop my mother from doing what she wanted to do once she set her mind to it—like finding me a new house. My best course of action was to just nod and agree. Or change the subject.

"Have you heard anything about Philip Grenville being in town?"

Lips pursed, she nodded. "He came by for a cup of coffee this morning. Linda Faye served him, and we were all polite, but I didn't want to be. I haven't seen him in years. He's really aged. Looks older than he should, and no wonder. Pervert."

"Did you tell Abbie?" How would she feel being so

close to her wedding and having her ex-husband show up?

"No. I haven't seen her since he came. Really, why would it be important? That man broke her heart." Ma drew herself up in indignant anger, and Chris laughed in her arms. At least he couldn't understand her words. "Her book should have been about a woman killing her ex-husband instead of a man killing his ex-wife."

"Ma!" I glanced around the shop, hoping the lull in conversations was coincidence and not customers trying to eavesdrop.

"Well, nobody could have blamed Abbie if she'd shot Philip dead. He deserved it years ago. Now she's finally got a chance at happiness with Eric. He's such a nice man. A good man. A successful man."

She sounded a little bit like the Jewish matchmaker in *Fiddler on the Roof.*

Ma kissed the tip of Chris's nose. "I wouldn't have been surprised to hear that some relative of some woman Philip slept with shot him in the head."

I wasn't comfortable with the direction this conversation was going. I lowered my voice, hoping she'd take a hint. "So why is Philip in town? Do you know?"

"Like I told you," Ma said. "To ruin Abbie's wedding."

Someone walked up to the cash register, so Ma handed Chris back to me. He bleated in disappointment, and I stuck a pacifier in his mouth.

As Ma rang up the ticket, she looked over her shoulder at me. "He'd better not bother Abbie. That's all I have to say. Or you and I will pay him a visit, and I'll shoot him myself." Her voice was just as loud as it had been before.

"Well, let's hope he doesn't get killed." I forced a

laugh. "You'd be a prime suspect now. You really should be careful about what you say."

Ma waved at the customer as he left. "I'm *always* careful about what I say." She trounced over to the coffee machines.

Ah, the beauty of self-deception. I didn't bother to argue. It's my policy not to argue with someone who is always right.

April May Winters walked up to the register. "You have to admit it's weird timing, given Abbie's new book and her wedding. Maybe Philip thinks he can somehow get a cut of the money she's making."

I shook my head. "Unless an author is a big name, they don't make a lot."

April looked skeptical, but I knew for a fact that Abbie was barely making enough money to live.

"You want something to eat?" April May asked.

"Yeah, I do. A turkey club. And a Mountain Dew. And would you please hand me a sugar cookie for Chris?"

"Mountain Dew?" April asked with raised brows. "Not your regular coffee?"

I shook my head. "No. I've developed a new bad habit. Caffeine in the form of green sugary fizz."

A minute later, as she handed me a paper-wrapped cookie and the drink, face squished into a frown, she glanced over her shoulder at Ma. "If this keeps up with Gail and Doris, I'm going to look for another job."

I frowned. Gail had worked for Ma since she'd started her business. And April had been working here for several years. "You mean this isn't like one of their normal fights?"

She shook her head a smidgen and leaned toward me. "No. I'll tell you about it when I bring you your food."

I got a table and put Chris, whose mouth was still plugged with the pacifier, in a high chair and then dropped into my own chair. Although the dining room was full and people were back to talking again, the place seemed strange without the background of Ma and Gail tossing comments back and forth. I never thought I'd say it, but I missed them ganging up to snipe at me.

April was on her way to my table with my order when a big blue WWPS truck pulled up outside in the parking lot. When the blue-uniformed man leaped from the driver's side and strolled toward the shop door carrying a box, April stopped midstep to stare at him. As far as I could see, every other woman in the place turned to look, too. Even my mother.

"April!" I stage-whispered.

"Huh?" She ripped her gaze from him as he walked through the door.

"You're gaping."

"Oh. . .oh." She almost tripped hurrying with her tray to my table. After she set it down, she slipped into a chair, positioned so she could still see him. "Wow."

I had to admit, the man was fine. I should know. I'm married to a man who has the same kind of effect on women. Still, this guy. . .

"He's new," April said. "His name is Clark."

"As in Clark Kent? Like Superman?"

"Mmm." April smiled. "But his last name is Matthews."

I checked him out. He did have a certain resemblance to the man of steel. I wondered if this was the same guy who had broken open the bags of kitty litter at Adler's Pet Emporium. He and my mother were in conversation at the counter. He told her how good her coffee was and that he could never get enough. Her angry persona melted. Then I heard her giggle. My mother never giggles.

While I wanted to stare at my mother's unusual behavior with the same freakish fascination with which a person rubbernecks at the aftermath of a car wreck, I had to find out from April what was going on with Ma and Gail, so I tore my attention from the front of the shop and put it on April. Chris slapped his chair with open palms and rocked back and forth.

"What's with Gail and Ma?"

"What?" She turned dreamy, unseeing eyes toward me.

I snapped my fingers in front of her face. "Come on, April. Snap out of it."

She blinked. "Oh. Sorry."

I leaned toward her. "If you like him so much, why don't you go say hello?"

"Oh, I couldn't do that. He's just too. . .well. . .*no way*."

This did not sound like the April I knew, but whatever. "All right. Then tell me what's going on with Gail and Ma."

April tensed and finally met my eyes directly. "They're fighting. Over Linda."

"Linda?"

"Yeah. Linda Faye King. Your mom hired her part-time to help early in the mornings because Gail has to temporarily come in two hours late. Linda is also helping to cater Abbie's wedding reception. Gail is really mad."

"Why?"

April shrugged. "I don't know. Gail won't say. Linda

always seemed nice to me, although sometimes she seems to be living in another dimension."

"How did Ma end up hiring her?" I asked.

"She was here at the right time when your mother was superbusy. Gail hadn't come in yet. She has to take her granddaughter to school right now. Well, Linda's gotten into real estate and comes in here every morning to get coffee. She overheard your mom talking about needing some temporary help in the morning. She needs some extra cash."

Chris spit out his pacifier and began to cry. I gave him the sugar cookie. I'm not above bribing my kids with sweets to get them to cooperate.

April glanced over my shoulder, and her eyes widened.

I turned around to see what she was looking at, and lo and behold, Clark was approaching our table.

"Hey, April."

She gaped up at him with an open mouth and said nothing, so I kicked her under the table.

"Uh. . ." She inhaled. "Hi."

He smiled. The man had it. Whatever "it" was. Like Max. But unlike Max, Clark seemed to know the effect he had on women and used it.

"You doin' okay, April?" Clark stretched, showing off his biceps.

"Uh-huh," she grunted.

"Well, good." His gaze lingered on her, and he rolled back and forth on his black walking shoes.

He had a copy of Abbie's book in his hand. Since April was stunned into silence, I thought I'd fill the gap to give her time to recover.

"Are you going to read that?" I asked.

His gaze slid to me, as if seeing me for the first time, and the fingers of his empty hand drummed a spastic rhythm on his thigh. He glanced down at the book and shook his head. "No. It's for my mom. She's a big mystery reader, and she's been waiting for this one."

"Does she live around here?" I asked.

"Yep. I just moved her into a house outside of town. She hasn't been well, and I'm taking care of her."

"Wow." April drew out the word, making it sound as though Clark had done something supermanly heroic. "That's so nice of you."

I bit my lip to keep from laughing. The man was only doing what most people normally do.

He preened a little bit and shrugged. "Gotta watch out for family, you know."

"Wow," April repeated.

I had a sudden thought that might help April out. "You know what? Abbie Grenville, the author of that book, is my best friend. I could get a bookplate for that book personally autographed for your mother. Then I could deliver it to your house." *With April in tow.*

"Now that would be really nice," he said. "My mother's name is Eunice Matthews."

April stared at him with rapt attention. I was tempted to look more closely to see if she was drooling.

"Well, I guess I'll see you later." He winked at April, waved, turned on his heel, and strolled out of the shop.

I thought April had stopped breathing again. I patted her arm. "It's okay. He only said hello. He didn't declare his undying love or anything." I paused. "Okay, well, he didn't really say hello; he said, 'Hey, April.' "

"I know." She took a deep breath, which relieved me. I had been afraid she was going to faint. "Wow." She turned glazed eyes toward me. "He knows my name."

"April!" Gail hollered. "We need you over here."

"Gail knows your name, too," I murmured.

April stood up, mumbled good-bye to me, and floated back to work. At least she'd been distracted from looking for another job.

As I ate my sandwich, I watched my mother and Gail. They were making wide swaths around each other to avoid accidentally touching, and there was no eye contact between them at all. When they did speak, their words were clipped and harsh. I found myself wishing one of them would just turn to the other and say something nice. Like I'd felt when I observed Jaylene and Henry.

A simple effort on the part of just one of them could end the ongoing hostility.

2

As I turned the key in the SUV, my cell phone rang from the depths of my purse. I flung pens, receipts, and other things aside as I dug for it. As was my habit, I didn't bother to look at the screen to check the caller ID.

I jammed the phone against my ear. "Hello?"

"Patricia?"

Only one person in the world calls me by my given name. Lady Angelica Louise Carmichael Cunningham, otherwise known as my mother-in-law.

"Hello, Angelica." Despite my best efforts not to be intimidated, I always find myself speaking more properly with her.

"How are you, dear?"

"I'm fine. How are you?" Angelica never calls me without a reason, so I stiffened in preparation for whatever she was going to say.

"I'm well. How are the children?"

"Everyone is good." I opened the center console in the SUV and pawed through the contents, looking for a headset. I found cleansing wipes, a bottle of germ killer, pens, fast-food napkins, and a slightly used mint. Where was my headset? "The kids are fine. So is Max."

I heard her brief intake of breath and braced myself for what she would say next. "Has Sammie stopped indulging in her unfortunate. . .habit?"

I dropped the lid on the console. It bounced once then shut.

"Mamamamamamamama," Chris chanted from his car seat.

"What's that noise?" Angelica asked. "Are you still there?"

"It's Chris. I'm here." Talking with gritted teeth and stiff lips is nearly impossible.

"Did you hear my question? Has Sammie—"

"Sammie is fine," I said, trying to force my jaw muscles to relax.

"I've spoken to some of my friends and found the name of a child psychiatrist."

This is a test, I told myself. *Only a test.* Chris was smacking his hands on his car seat in rhythm with his repetitious monosyllable. Perhaps he was destined to be a drummer.

"Patricia?"

I took a deep breath. "Sammie is going to be fine. She's just developed a habit of picking things up off the floor and putting them in her pockets. It's not a big deal. She's—"

"Kleptomania is a serious mental disorder, dear."

"Klepto. . .what are you saying? What exactly did Max tell you she's doing?"

"Stealing," Angelica said.

I knew my husband would never say such a thing. He had agreed with me that it was probably just a phase. At least that's what he told me.

"She's *not* stealing," I said. "She's a neatnik. She just picks things up off the ground and the floor."

"And puts them in her pockets!" Angelica sighed long and hard. "Sometimes it takes longer for mothers to see the truth about their children."

Well, that might be an accurate statement, but I happen to know that a person's version of the truth can be subjective, based on their perception of reality. And that was the big problem here. Angelica and I rarely perceived reality the same way.

"Sammie says she's worried about Chris," I said. "This didn't start until he began trying to crawl. Unfortunately, Sammie watched a show where a toddler choked to death on something he got off the floor."

"Whatever you believe, dear, but this is why she needs a distraction. Have you made a decision?"

She was referring to the kitten, and I wouldn't let myself be fooled by her use of the endearment. She used words like weapons, wielding them like friendly fire that kills just as dead as enemy fire. I decided to play with her head.

"A decision? Um, about what?"

I heard her delicate sigh. "About the cat, dear. Maxwell said he's leaving it all up to you. . ." Her voice trailed off.

Which I don't understand at all. . . I completed her sentence in my head. "Oh yes. The cat." I paused just long enough to irritate her. "Yes, I've made a decision."

"And?" Her tone of voice changed. "This. . .is important. Not just for Sammie."

That was an odd statement for her to make. Was that vulnerability I heard in her voice? I felt a niggle of guilt. Playing with her head—anybody's head—wasn't nice. And the Lord had been trying to teach me to be nice for a long time now. I had only to look at the Adlers to see the end result of not being kind to someone.

"I've decided that Sammie can have the cat."

"Good." Relief laced the satisfaction in her voice. "She needs to pick which kitten she wants from the litter. She gets first choice."

"Why now?" I asked. "They aren't ready to leave their mother yet."

"That's the way it's done, dear," Angelica said. "What time this afternoon after she gets home from school is good? Hayley will be home after we play tennis."

Give someone an inch, and they'll take a mile, as my mother would say. I'd given my mother-in-law just the tiniest bit of leverage by agreeing to the kitten, and now she was taking over, which she'd do in every area of my life if I let her. Just like my mother. But unlike my mother, Angelica doesn't believe I'm good enough to be a Cunningham, along with my many other failures of character. Unfortunately, I resent that.

"Patricia?"

"Tell Hayley around four."

Angelica said good-bye and I hung up, wondering how I got into these things. My life was being controlled by two domineering women, not to mention all the demands from my family. I felt like I was losing myself.

I needed to go back to work. That's all there was to it. Not to the self-storage business. When I left there, we turned the running of daily operations over to our office manager, Shirl. She was doing a great job. We'd even hired help for her.

But maybe I could get a job in another part of the Cunningham family business. Max and his father had recently begun work on a housing development. Perhaps I could help with that. For the first time since I'd gotten up that morning, I felt a twinge of excitement.

━━━

The trees had shed most of their leaves, helped by the strong wind I felt pushing at my SUV as I drove to the cat breeder's place.

I'd texted Max on my cell phone and told him what was going on. Lately we'd developed the habit of text messaging on our phones rather than calling. I enjoyed the new technology. Plus, if he was in a meeting, he could still subtly check his message and even answer me—unlike answering a ringing phone.

Sammie and I stopped briefly at the local Gas 'n' Go to get some juice for her and to satisfy my latest addiction, an ice-cold, bubbly Mountain Dew from the fountain. After that, I continued on to Hayley Whitmore's house. In the backseat, Sammie babbled about cats and school. Fortunately, her presence kept Chris entertained.

"Mommy, look!" Sammie bounced and pointed at a farm we were passing.

A big sign loomed in the field, advertising a cornfield maze. We'd done the maze the last couple of years and enjoyed it.

"Can we go?" she asked.

"We'll talk to Daddy tonight," I said. "I'm sure we can."

Hayley's house was near the Cunningham estate. The Cunninghams had moved to this neighborhood when Max was a teenager. . . . Well, this wasn't a neighborhood like the typical suburban sprawl. Instead, large houses were planted tastefully on acres of carefully manicured land. It was beautiful.

Despite my irritation with Ma for going behind my back to set up house-hunting help, it *was* true that we were considering a new home. Our present home still seemed crowded with the addition of a very active baby, even though my oldest stepson, Tommy, was away at college. My in-laws wanted me and Max to buy property out here, build a home, and be near them. I figured it wasn't because my mother-in-law particularly wanted me nearer to her, but it was more likely that she wanted to make sure the children were raised correctly. More of her influence and less of mine.

I knew Max would like being nearer to his father. He sounded a little nostalgic when he mentioned houses and land for sale in this neighborhood. I tried to act interested, but I couldn't imagine living here. In addition to being closer to my in-laws, living here would mean being farther from my parents and everything I'd known my whole life. Besides, I wouldn't fit in. I was a farm girl. A redneck through and through. Despite the fact that I married a man with money, my clothes still usually came from the racks in Wal-Mart. There was no way I would join the country club and meet the girls twice a week. I hated tennis and golf.

Still. . .was I being selfish?

I found Hayley's place easily because the shiny brass street numbers glowed on an ornate black mailbox. Following the curved, tree-lined driveway, I calculated in my head how much the asphalt had cost. After I rounded a final bend, I saw the house, and my breath caught in my throat. Built in the style of a southern mansion with tall white pillars gracing the front, the building glowed in the setting sun. I felt like donning a Civil War–style gown and saying, *Tara! Home. I'll go home.* Just call me Scarlett.

I parked in the circular driveway, half expecting servants to run from the house to help us from the SUV. Then I turned to Sammie, who was eagerly undoing her seat belt. "Honey, don't pick up anything in the house and put it in your pocket, okay?"

"I know, Mommy." I could hear the sigh in her answer.

She jumped from the car, coat flapping around her legs, more excited than I'd seen her in a long time. As much as I hated to think it, perhaps Angelica had been partially right. Sammie needed a distraction. A new addition to a family, especially one as demanding as Chris, was hard on everyone. And sometimes the kids who are the quietest get lost in the process.

While she ran over to the flower bed full of lovely mums and other fall plantings, I took Chris from his car seat and balanced him on my hip. He started yanking on my hair, messing up the already frizzy blond curls.

When our motley crew was assembled on the massive veranda, I rang the bell and didn't have to wait long. A petite girl, about my height, answered. For a moment, I thought she was a teenager; then I realized this was Hayley. I was surprised by her youth. I had expected she would be older since she was friends with my mother-in-law. Hayley wore a pair of jeans and a black sweater set with pretty gold buttons. I'm small, but I'd gained way too much weight when I was pregnant with Chris—and I still hadn't lost it all. She made me feel frowsy.

"Hayley?" I asked.

"You must be Trish." She looked me up and down and then smiled. The smile was genuine and reached her eyes with warmth that surprised me. "It's nice to meet someone as short as I am. Come on in."

We stepped into the marble-floored foyer. She took our coats and draped them on an antique umbrella stand, and we followed her into a central main hallway. The mellow oak floors looked like refurbished antique wood. Two rooms extended from the hall; one looked like a music room complete with a grand piano. The other was a living room.

Chris babbled, motioning with his arms that he wanted to get down. I jiggled him up and down.

"This is Chris, and this is Sammie." I pressed my free hand on Sammie's head, trying to send a mental message to behave and be good. I needn't have worried. Sammie beamed up at Hayley.

"Thank you for the kitty," she said.

I couldn't have scripted it better myself.

"Oh, aren't you just the sweetie. Your grandmother has already told me all about you. She just loves her grandchildren so much." Hayley glanced at me. "Your in-laws have been over here to dinner recently. We've really hit it off."

I felt a twinge of guilt. Angelica wanted to see the kids more often. I just couldn't stand her attitude toward me. But was I depriving my kids of something they really should have just because I didn't want to deal with her? My mother was just as judgmental of me in her own way, yet our family spent a lot of time at her house.

Hayley took Sammie's hand. "Let's go to the back where you can play with the kittens and decide which one you want."

She motioned for me to follow her.

Two whitish-gray cats with dark-tipped ears, feet, and tails slipped from the living room and dashed in front of me. I noticed a third sitting on top of a bookshelf in the hallway, tail twitching as it watched me walk past. I began to feel like eyes were staring at me from the walls. All my good feelings about doing this for Sammie slipped away, and I wondered if I should have said no. Cats were sneaky. Cats were sly. Cats were. . .

A horrid wail came from somewhere in the house. I skidded to a stop. It sounded like a baby with hormone issues.

"What is that?" I asked.

Hayley looked around at me, then up and down the hall. "I think that was Mr. Chang Lee."

"Mr. Chang Lee?" I pictured a Chinese cook suffering an acute case of appendicitis.

"Yes. My retired champion Siamese. He's the first cat I ever bought. I guess he got out of his room. He's an escape artist."

"Is he sick?"

She stared at me with raised brows. "Sick?"

"He sounds like he's dying."

She laughed. "Heavens, no. That's just the way Siamese cats talk."

My stomach clenched. "Do they all sound like that?"

"To one degree or another. Some are more vocal than others." She laughed again. "Listen, watch yourself. Mr.

Lee doesn't like most people except me."

Nervous, I glanced around. "What will he do?"

"Sometimes he attacks people's legs. He's gotten my husband, Leighton, several times, but they've learned to avoid each other. I try to keep Mr. Lee locked up when strangers are here."

Sammie giggled. I wasn't amused. While she chatted with Hayley, I was on the lookout for an attack cat. Then I glanced up at the cat on the bookshelf. Would it leap down on my head as I walked by? It opened its mouth and yowled.

The noises of the cats rattled my brain. Strange for someone who easily tuned out the complaining of an almost-toddler. What if the kitten Sammie picked out was the most vocal of the litter?

I felt something bump up against my leg. I jumped back and looked down into the bluest cat eyes I'd ever seen. The animal had materialized out of nowhere. It looked up at me, opened its mouth, and wailed.

Hayley turned. "Ah, there he is. Mr. Lee." She paused and stared speculatively at me. "Wow, Trish. You're special. He likes you. I've never known that to happen before." She leaned down and scratched his head. "Oh, my whittle kitty," she murmured. "You mama's baby boy, honey bunny?"

I thought I might be sick. Mr. Lee purred.

"Kitty's messy wessy," Hayley said and then straightened and looked at me. "Mr. Lee tends to spread cat litter all over. I'm not sure why. It annoys my husband."

It would annoy me, too. Mr. Lee began rubbing his face on my ankles. There was indeed cat litter on the floor.

Great. I hoped our new cat didn't have the same habit. I gently tried to shove him away with my foot, but he stuck like glue, and I was afraid to push the issue, given what Hayley said about his attack tendencies. "Being liked isn't all it's cracked up to be," I mumbled at her.

Hayley laughed. "Oh, wow. You really are funny. Angelica tells me that all the time. Now I understand what she means." She looked down at Sammie. "Okay, now let's go pick out your kitten."

I didn't think Hayley had the right idea about what my mother-in-law meant when she said I was funny, but I wasn't going to explain.

"Angelica is one of the nicest people I know," Hayley said over her shoulder. "She's been good to me. We play tennis regularly. It's just like her to do something sweet like buy a kitten for Sammie."

I wanted to ask her if she had the right Angelica. But she did, of course. Hayley was the kind of woman my mother-in-law had wanted Max to marry. The kind of woman he was married to the first time around. When he married me, Angelica wasn't happy and had always let me know I wasn't quite good enough, thus leading to our present impasse.

On my truly honest days, I admitted to myself that though Angelica's attitude bothered me, I did crave a better relationship with her, but I was clueless as to how to go about getting it.

The cat kept wrapping himself between my feet, and I was having trouble walking.

"Cacacacaca," Chris said, staring at the cat and beating in rhythm with his heel on my leg.

"He's adorable," Hayley said. "I really want children. . . but. . .anyway, maybe someday."

She sounded so wistful that I couldn't help but wonder why they hadn't had any.

We finally reached the back of the house and entered what might have been a family room or a great room—emphasis on "great." Mr. Lee was still pasted to my ankles, but I was momentarily distracted from his attentions by the floor-to-ceiling windows and french doors that covered the wall in front of me. Doors framed by long, striped, sateen curtains led outside to a pool. Well, *pool* is too mundane a word to describe what I saw. This was an artistic creation. Abstract shape, rocks, a waterfall, and a Jacuzzi. I was wowed.

"Mommy, look!" Sammie squealed. "What a pretty pond."

"Swimming pool," I murmured.

Chris squirmed in my arms. "Down," he said firmly, using one of five words he said very clearly.

"No," I told him with an equally firm tone. That was one of his other words, and he learned it from me.

"But it's got rocks," Sammie said. "How can it be a pool?"

"That's part of the decorating." Hayley was staring out the windows. "We just had that put in."

"It's beautiful." As Chris squirmed in my arms, I thought how nice it would be to have a Jacuzzi to relax in and a pool for the kids.

"I've always wanted one," Hayley said. She pointed to a stack of shiny house-decorating magazines and books sitting next to a leaded-glass vase filled with red roses on a glass and iron coffee table. "Leighton did it for me. I wanted to landscape around the pool. See?" She picked up a heavy book, the front of which was illustrated with a pool very similar to hers, surrounded by a garden that would take at least part-time help to maintain. "Isn't it great? I bought this book last weekend to show Leighton what I want to do with the landscaping." Her eyes moved from the pool back to me. "I hope we don't have to move. Anyway, the kittens are in the laundry room. You want to come with me?"

Chris whimpered in frustration, and I jiggled him up and down on my hip as I followed her. Then I noticed the spectacular fireplace, lined with bookcases on both sides, filled mostly with the latest fiction.

A single picture graced the mantel. I went over to look more closely, trying not to step on Mr. Lee, who was no longer wrapped around my ankles but still hanging close by.

"Your wedding?" I pointed at a picture of Hayley in a gown next to a man who looked to be thirty years her senior.

"Yes. That's Leighton." She picked up the picture. "That's from our wedding."

"Did you get married outside?"

"Yes." She set down the photo. "At a botanical garden. We haven't been married long."

"Where are you from?" I asked.

"New York City."

In the picture, Hayley was smiling and holding on to Leighton's hand.

"Your wedding gown was amazing," I said. "My best

friend is getting married in a little more than two weeks."

"Really? How exciting. To be in love and have the whole world in front of you." Hayley's eyes sparkled for a moment. Then her gaze became unfocused, and she chewed her bottom lip. Finally, she blinked and stared clearly at me. "Does she live around here?"

I nodded. "Yes. Her name is Abbie Grenville."

"Do you mean that author person?"

"That's the one."

"Mommy, can we see the kittens now, please?" Sammie whispered.

Poor thing. She was trying so hard to behave even though she was nearly vibrating in her excitement.

"Oh sure, honey," Hayley said, taking her hand again. "We'll look at them right now." She glanced at me over her shoulder. "I think I saw your friend this weekend at the fall festival."

"Yes, she had a book signing there. I was there early, helping her set up."

"We were there right around lunch. I was going to look at her book, but Leighton was impatient to leave. He has to eat at regular times. And he only eats certain things."

I followed Hayley through a large gourmet kitchen complete with black granite countertops and cherry cabinets. She opened another door at the far end, revealing a long hallway. I happened to look down at the floor and noticed that Mr. Lee had disappeared.

"I'm getting lost," Sammie mumbled.

Hayley laughed. I understood. This was a lot of house.

Walking down the hall, we passed a room on the left that looked to be a man's study, traditionally decorated in hunter green. Sunlight streamed in through large leaded windows. Two walls were lined with floor-to-ceiling book-shelves. Several display cabinets filled with guns lined a third wall.

"Your husband's office?"

"Yes," Hayley said.

"Does your husband hunt?" I asked.

"Yes. He's even been on safaris." Hayley gave an exaggerated shiver.

I wasn't paying much attention to her. All I could think about was how Max would love a study like this.

"Ggggg." Chris bobbed up and down in my arms, pointing with his chubby finger. I realized he was telling me that Hayley and Sammie were walking away. I hurried after them as they turned into a room on the right, a large laundry room.

The room was amazing. A woman's dream. Wallpaper with climbing vines decorated the walls. A top-of-the-line washer and dryer were surrounded by built-in shelves and cupboards. There was even a phone/intercom system on the wall. A silky-looking Siamese cat perched on the edge of the dryer next to an open box containing several of Jaylene's Kitty Kollers. The cardboard looked like it had been caught in a tape explosion. Jaylene must have been in a frenzy the day she mailed that one out.

Sammie was squatting on the floor next to a terry-lined basket that held five kittens. "Mommy, look," she said.

I had to admit the almost-all-white kittens were adorable.

"Cacacacaca," Chris yelled in my ear as he tried to throw himself from my arms onto the floor. No doubt I would be diagnosed with child-induced hearing loss later in life.

"Will the kittens stay white?" I gasped as I tried to hang on to my hefty son.

"No. They'll start developing gray points soon." Hayley knelt next to Sammie, gently explaining things to her.

I glanced at the rapt expression on my daughter's face and knew absolutely that I'd made the right decision despite my own doubts.

Hayley stood to let Sammie decide which kitten she wanted.

"Does your husband help you with the cats?" I asked Hayley, speaking loudly over Chris's protests.

"Yes. . . ." She frowned. "Well, he did. Right now he's awfully busy. He's thinking about a couple of job offers. But he's promised he'll help me again."

I thought Hayley seemed a little defensive in telling me so much, and I wondered if things were as good as she claimed.

"Caaaa," Chris wailed, pointing at the kittens with his fist.

I jiggled him harder, and as his cries wavered back and forth from loud to louder, I encouraged Sammie to hurry. She finally decided. How, I'll never know, because they all looked alike to me.

Hayley complimented Sammie on her choice and put a tiny blue ribbon on the kitten's neck. Then we followed her back through the house, twisting and turning our way to the front door.

There Mr. Lee materialized as if by magic and was once again glued to my foot. Hayley noticed and smiled.

"You should feel privileged, Trish. I've never known him to do that with a stranger."

I stared down at the cat, trying to communicate my desire for him to leave me alone. *My mother taught me that getting up close and personal with someone I don't know without an invitation is bad manners.*

I was shocked when the cat met my gaze, yowled, twined around my ankles a few times, then strolled to Hayley and sat on his haunches next to her, staring at me. Was he mocking me?

Hayley handed us our coats.

As I bundled up Chris, Hayley looked down at Sammie then back at me.

"You can bring her back to visit the kitten." Her face grew wistful. "You can come often."

That's when I realized Hayley was lonely. I felt bad for her. Although I do believe money can make life easier, it can't take the place of people.

As I put the children in the car, a black BMW streaked up the driveway, pulling around the side of the house. I assumed that was Leighton, and my hunch was confirmed when the man I recognized from the picture on Hayley's mantel walked back around the house.

I waved, and he approached me.

"Hello," he said. "I assume you're Trish Cunningham. Hayley said you were coming this afternoon."

"Yes." I offered him my hand, and he shook it.

Leighton Whitmore's photo hadn't done him justice. He was as tall as Max and good-looking in a way that age doesn't impact. A mere photograph could never reveal the full extent of his charisma. Especially when he smiled like he was doing now.

"Angelica and Andrew have told us all about you, and your husband speaks highly of you."

I smiled even as I wondered when Leighton had met Max. "It's nice to meet you."

"And you, as well," he said. He bent down and spoke to the children. We exchanged a few more pleasantries, then he disappeared inside.

As I pulled down the driveway, I wondered if they were truly happy. Hayley didn't seem to be. I had a fleeting thought that perhaps Angelica recognized Hayley's loneliness, and that was the reason she invited Hayley to do things. Then I dismissed it. Angelica would never be that sensitive.

I called Abbie as soon as I got home, but she couldn't talk. She was on the phone with Eric, who was out of town. I didn't want to interrupt them. Philip's presence in town could wait.

I answered some e-mails, including one from my oldest stepson, Tommy, and another from Eric's daughter, Sherry, who was Tommy's girlfriend—a relationship that had continued after both of them graduated from high school.

Tommy was away at college. He'd had a last-minute change of majors and was studying criminal justice, much to Max's parents' dismay. They wanted him to be a lawyer.

That reminded me of Angelica's opinion about Sammie. I needed Max to assure me that he didn't really think Sammie had a dark future as a kleptocriminal in some prison cell, but he was ensconced in his study.

I glanced at my watch. It was late, and I didn't have time to make dinner. I ordered pizza instead, ignoring the tug of guilt I felt for not planning ahead. While I waited for it to be delivered, I paced the house feeling vaguely restless. Not that I didn't have a lot to do. I had bookkeeping to do for Max. A house to keep. I also had the never-ending piles of laundry. I even had a stack of books from the library, but I wasn't interested in any of them. Frankly, I was just bored.

Most of the women I knew at church were content to be at home or at least wished they could be home. Knowing that piled more guilt on my head because I wasn't content. That made me a failure in my eyes. Aren't all women supposed to adore taking care of their families full-time?

I wandered back into the kitchen. Sammie had tossed her coat on the back of a chair. I picked it up, ready to hang it on a peg next to the back door, but I felt something hard in the pocket. I reached inside and pulled out a squashed, unopened pack of gum and a rock that looked very similar to the rocks in Hayley's flower beds. The package of gum looked like it had been run over by a truck and probably came from the parking lot at the Gas 'n' Go. At least it wasn't used, but it still grossed me out, and I tossed it in the trash. Then I balanced the rock in my palm.

A rock is no big deal, I told myself. Kids always pick up stuff like rocks. But a little voice in the back of my head asked me if maybe Angelica was right. And worse, it told me if I were a better mother and more content maybe Sammie wouldn't have kleptomaniacal tendencies.

"Mom!" Charlie yelled from the family room. "I can't hear Mike over Chris." My middle son spent hours each day on his cell phone with his best friend, Mike. Anyone who says males don't talk as much as females is seriously unobservant. It's just the topics that differ.

I realized my youngest son had been noisy for a while. I'd tuned him out because the sounds were the whiny kind of talking he did for self-entertainment and not because he was in need or wanted attention. I could tell the difference, so I had learned to ignore the noise. Not everyone in the family had the same ability.

I went into the family room, scooped Chris out of his activity center, and carried him with me to the kitchen, where I stuck him in a high chair and covered his round cheeks with kisses. He beamed at me. Something crunched under my feet as I walked to the counter, but I ignored it, not wanting to be reminded of my housekeeping failures. As I cut up a banana for him, I heard the soft padding of bare feet behind me. I turned and saw Max.

"Hey, I really need to talk to you," I said.

"Dadadadadadadada," Chris said, holding out his arms.

Max took Chris's hands in his and blew on them, making whooshing sounds. Chris chortled. Then Max looked at me. "I heard the little guy yakking. I have a feeling he's always going to be vocal."

I smiled. "Probably."

Max came over and snaked his arms around my waist, and I leaned back against him.

Then I felt him shift back and forth. "What's on the floor?"

We both looked down. Me with dread, thinking it had to be Cheerios or something the kids had dropped.

"Is that. . .gravel?" he asked, wiggling his toes.

"No-o-o." I reached down and scooped up a familiar substance. "It's kitty litter. Must have been stuck in my shoes. I have new trainers, and they have deep treads."

While I swept up the pieces of litter, I told him about buying supplies from Adler's Pet Emporium and the hole in the litter bag. Then about our visit to Hayley's house.

"Mother told me you decided Sammie could have the cat." He kissed the top of my head. "Thank you."

I pulled myself from his grasp and turned around. "Do you mean you were worried I would say no?"

"Not worried," he said. "Just hoping you would do it for. . .well, for my mother. . .and Sammie."

"To avoid conflict and hard feelings, you mean?"

"Something like that." He pushed a piece of hair away from my face.

"Well, I'm struggling with hard feelings today." I crossed my arms. "Did you tell your mother that Sammie was stealing?"

The drop of his jaw told me all I needed to know.

"That's what I thought," I said. "I just needed to know for sure."

"I can't remember exactly what I did say, but whatever it was, that wasn't anywhere near the word I used. I can't imagine where she got the idea."

"She called it kleptomania and said she's found a really good psychiatrist for Sammie."

Max shook his head. "I'll talk to her."

"And your mother isn't the only one who's taking over. My mother talked to a real estate agent for us. Linda Faye King. Remember the emergency room nurse? She's into real estate now."

"What?" He raised his eyebrows. "Have we decided to move?"

I shrugged. "Not that I know of, but everybody is making decisions for me. My mother. Your mother. As usual. So I just go along with it all."

He smiled. "You *pretend* to go along with it and then just quietly do what you want to do."

I considered that and frowned. "That's a bit passive-aggressive, isn't it?"

He laughed. "No. Not in you. You just avoid making scenes, which is a good thing, as far as I'm concerned."

"Oh. Okay." I stared up into his green eyes. "I had a fleeting thought today about living out near your parents."

Surprise lit his face, making his eyes greener. "Really?"

"The cat breeder lives out there. Hayley Whitmore. Her house is too huge for my taste, but I liked the deck and the pool."

"Whitmore? Leighton and Hayley?"

"Yep," I said. "And Leighton said you know him."

"I've met him through my father." A quick frown wrinkled Max's forehead, and then it slipped away. "Anyway, you liked their house?"

"Not *their* house. It was way too pretentious. Like Tara from *Gone with the Wind*. But I just thought about you and how happy you'd be out there and. . ."

He kissed me soundly on the lips, and I felt it down to

my toes. When he was done, he stepped back and smiled while I pulled myself together. He knows what he does to me.

"So we can, um, talk about it," I finally said when my heart slowed.

"We don't have to decide right now," he said.

I heard the back door open, and Karen, my step-daughter, rushed into the kitchen from work, her long hair swinging in her face.

"Caaaaaaaa," Chris squealed.

Karen dropped a kiss on his head and then looked at us. "Dad. Mom." She dropped a bag of pretzels on the table and reached for the refrigerator door. After a quick look inside the fridge, she slammed the door. "What's for dinner?"

"Pizza," I said.

"Pizza again?" She screwed her pretty face into a frown.

Even my kids were heaping burning coals of guilt on my head.

"Yes, *again*." I tried not to snarl, and I also avoided Max's eyes in case he felt the same way Karen did.

Charlie exploded into the kitchen from the other direction, clinging to his cell phone and just missing ramming into Karen.

"Watch it, moron," she said.

Charlie stuck his tongue out at her.

"Stop now, you two, before you get started," Max warned.

She rolled her eyes. Charlie grinned and turned to me and Max, waving his phone in our faces.

"Mike's brother got caught today with drugs. He's in

big trouble. It's called estisee."

"Ecstasy," Karen said. "And he's a moron, too. I see him at the mall all the time."

"Karen. . ." Max met her gaze, and she tightened her lips into a thin line.

"He's in such big trouble," Charlie said. "Grounded for life." He bounced out of the kitchen.

I was glad that Mike's parents were taking a hard stand.

"Dadadadada," Chris intoned from his high chair.

"I see him at the mall with a group of kids he goes to junior college with. At least there will be one less idiot loose in the mall." Karen sniffed. Max cleared his throat, and she tossed her hair. "You gotta admit it's stupid."

Well, we couldn't really argue with her point. And with that proclamation, she asked me to call her when the pizza arrived, mumbled about tons of homework, and disappeared down the hall.

I had to admit I was jealous. Karen had a life. She got out of the house.

I wrapped my arms around Max. "Honey, I think I want to go back to work part-time. Outside the home."

He blinked in surprise. "Where? Back at Self-Storage?"

"No." I looked up at him. "Shirl's doing fine managing everything. I need something else."

His expression was wistful. "I kind of thought you were happy at home."

Sometimes men are clueless. They see only what they want to see. Max liked me being home. He's old-fashioned that way. His mother was always home when he was young. Not that she was the typical suburban housewife type—well, she was typical for her social class. That meant lunch at the club after a nice game of tennis. She had no money worries, so she could do that. But she was "home."

I had no money worries, either. If I wanted to, I could go enjoy a nice game of tennis with my mother-in-law, but I don't like tennis.

"I'm happy enough, but I miss the social interaction. I miss the regimentation. I miss having a purpose."

"Taking care of our home and kids isn't purpose enough?" he asked.

"Would it be for you?" I thought I had him there.

"Chris is getting on your nerves, isn't he? It's the teething thing."

Max wasn't getting it. Or he didn't want to. "No. I just ignore Chris's grumpiness. That's not it. I just want to get out." I took a deep breath. "I had a really good thought. How about I work for your company?"

He stepped back, surprise lighting his eyes again. "You mean, work for Cunningham and Son?"

"Well, your dad is semiretired. Seems to me you could use a partner."

Max blinked like a toad in a hailstorm.

"What's wrong?" I frowned at him. "You wouldn't want to work with me? You worked with me at Storage part-time. I do bookkeeping work for you here at home. You don't think I could do it?"

"Well, it's not that, exactly. . . ." He started to back away from me.

"You're afraid of what your parents will think?"

"No. . . ."

I planted my fists on my hips. "Is it because I didn't go to Harvard?"

"Um, no. . . ."

"Well, what is it, then?"

"I'm not sure—"

The doorbell rang. The pizza had arrived.

"I'll go get that," Max said and quickly left the room.

"Fine," I grumbled, my feelings hurt. I thought maybe he'd go with my idea. Especially after I held out the olive branch of living near his parents.

On Tuesday afternoon, I prepared to meet Abbie and my mother at the church hall. Abbie was supposed to get there earlier than us to fiddle with the decorations she was going to use. As I passed through my kitchen on the way to the garage, the yellow walls glowed, and I felt just as radiant. Max had come home early so he could watch the little kids for me while I was gone. But he'd come home before the time we'd discussed and managed to sidetrack me. Not that he has to work hard to sidetrack me. But as a result, I had totally forgiven him of his insensitivity the night before and even felt hopeful. I figured I'd attack Max's doubts about me working at Cunningham and Son like water wearing away a rock. Slowly and over a period of time.

I was leaving a bit early in hopes of getting a chance to talk to Abbie at the fellowship hall before my mother got there. I tried to reach her by phone to tell her, but when I got her voice mail, I left a message confirming that Ma and I would see her shortly. I wanted to tell her about Philip.

I saw a sign for the Gas 'n' Go, which happens to be near the church hall. My mouth watered. Funny how addiction affects the body. I pulled into the parking lot and the debate began. *Must have Mountain Dew,* one voice in my head whispered. *Just say no,* another retorted. I sighed.

Then in my rearview mirror, I saw a WWPS truck whiz by on the road. That reminded me of Doris's Doughnuts and my mother. . .her constant nagging and how tired I got of people telling me what to do.

I ordered the voices in my head to be quiet, grabbed my official I GET MY GET-UP-'N'-GO FROM GAS 'N' GO plastic refillable cup, and climbed from my SUV. Inside, I nodded at Pat, the clerk, and headed straight for the soda machine, half expecting to see a little good imp and a little bad imp sitting on the counter ready to continue the argument.

As the fizzy liquid flowed over chipped ice in my cup, I told myself I needed to break the habit.

Back outside, I was climbing into my SUV when I heard the sound of a car window sliding down. Then someone called my name.

I turned and saw Linda Faye King in a tiny hybrid car parked right next to me. She looked totally put together in nicely cut brown slacks and a silky gold sweater. She tossed a leather briefcase on top of a jacket on the passenger seat.

"Hey," I said.

"I'm glad I caught you." She sounded a bit breathless. "I'm supposed to meet your mother at the reception hall, but I just got a call. I have to meet a real estate client. I drove by the church, but your mother wasn't there. She's not answering her cell phone, either. Can you tell her for me?"

"Yep. No problem." I took a sip of my drink. So good. Unfortunately, the word that came to mind was *ecstasy*.

"Oh." Linda reached into her purse and pulled out a gold business card holder with her red-tipped fingers. "You and I need to get together and discuss what you're looking for in a house. I have several listings now that might suit you." She handed me the card. "You can reach me at these numbers." A diamond tennis bracelet dangled from her wrist.

I wondered if the bracelet was a gift. It didn't look like the purchase of a newly minted real estate agent who needed a part-time job. "Okay," I said, even though I had no intention of following through. At least not right now.

We said our good-byes. Linda headed off in one direction, and I headed in the other toward the church hall. This wooded countryside wasn't developed. I saw FOR SALE signs along the road that I hadn't paid attention to before. Linda's name was on the bottom of each of them.

I pulled into the parking lot in front of the church fellowship hall. Ma and Abbie both attended this church. The congregation had recently bought this property and put up the building. Plans were in the works for a sanctuary to follow in the spring. But for now, the members used the multipurpose building for their worship services as well as social events, prayer meetings, and other group activities.

Backed up against the woods, the soft peach brick of the building glowed in the afternoon sun. Abbie wasn't here. I glanced at my watch and wondered where she was.

I rubbed my arms, feeling a tingle of excitement. My best friend since I was little was getting married. My matron of honor dress hung in my closet, and I couldn't wait to wear it. I'd been Abbie's maid of honor when she married Philip, but this time was different. This time I liked her husband-to-be, Eric Scott. I'd met him right after I found the body of Jim Bob Jenkins in the milk case of our local grocery store. Eric had been the lead detective in the murder investigation.

He'd pursued Abbie long and hard and finally convinced her to try again with him. A new chance for love.

Just as I stepped from my SUV and shut the door, my mother roared up in her catering van. I waited for her.

When she jerked her body from the vehicle, I knew something was wrong. "Hey, Ma. You—"

"I am just so mad I could spit nails." She slammed the door shut.

"I'm sorry. What's—"

"After all, it is *my* business, you know." She strode toward the building.

I followed in the wake of her hostility. "Yes, I—"

"And my name is on that sign. Big as day, it says 'Doris's Doughnuts.' " She stomped up the step to the cement walkway.

Breathlessly I joined her. "Yes, it—"

"That means *I'm the boss*." She glared at me, stuck the key in the lock, turned it, and flung open the door to the church hall, banging it on the side of the building. Then she stalked through the opening with me trailing behind her. "Where is Linda?"

"She can't make it," I gasped.

Ma paused. "What?"

"I saw her at the Gas 'n' Go. She asked me to tell you she had an emergency and can't make it. Something to do with a client."

"Well, that just makes my day complete." Ma strode to the kitchen area and began flinging open cupboards. "I hope the women in charge of the morning Bible study put everything back the way it's all supposed to be. They usually don't, you know. And they just had a luncheon."

She sniffed the air. "What is that smell?"

I shrugged and grunted. Saying anything was taking the risk of having my head bitten off. As Ma scurried around trying to find the source of the odor, I examined the kitchen. It was a cook's dream and a good indication of how important socializing was to the church members. There was plenty of counter space and cupboards. A large center island held an additional sink, which I couldn't fully see at the moment because of the bags that covered the surface.

On the edge of the island lay a copy of Abbie's new book. She had said she would be here earlier in the day to drop some things off and look at the supplies in the kitchen cupboards to make sure she didn't need to buy anything else.

I sneaked a look inside the bags and found packages of plain blue napkins, matching paper plates, and plastic cups, along with plastic flatware.

"It's the trash," Ma said.

I glanced up at her. "What?"

"The smell is coming from the trash." She snatched the plastic bag from the metal can, grumbling under her breath that she couldn't depend on anybody to help her.

"Do you want me to take that out?" I dropped the napkins back into the bag.

"No." Ma stomped across the tiled floor to the back door. "You try to find the punch bowl. Who knows where that is."

I heard the squeaky front door swing open. Both of us turned, and Abbie walked in carrying a drink from McDonald's.

"Well, at least the bride-to-be is faithful," Ma grumbled.

Abbie met my gaze with raised brows. Ma disappeared outside, and I heard her footsteps clomping down the stairs that led to the parking lot and yard behind the church.

"Hey," I said.

"Hi." Abbie crossed the room and kissed my cheek.

"Where were you? I thought you'd be here before me."

"I was." She dropped her coat on the counter, followed by a wool blazer with dull brass buttons.

I looked more closely at her. "Are you okay?"

"I'm fine." She brought the straw in her drink to her mouth and didn't meet my eyes. I didn't believe her reply. Her eyelids were red rimmed.

"Abbie, have you been crying?" An awful thought occurred to me. "Have you and Eric been fighting?"

She shook her head. "No. He's out of town, remember? At that training school." She took a deep breath and seemed to pull herself together. "Did you see the napkins?"

"Yep. Sort of. . .plain, aren't they?"

She half smiled. "Nothing formal. This wedding is going to be different from my first. I don't want to take any chance of. . .flashbacks."

I looked up at Abbie in time to see a quick frown crease her forehead, then it was gone. If I hadn't known her so well, I wouldn't have noticed it.

"That's probably a good idea. When you married Philip, it was a formal affair, all gold and white and perfect, and look how that turned out. But this is the real thing."

She thunked her half-finished drink on the counter and rubbed the middle of her forehead with her index finger.

"Are you okay, Abs? Do you have a headache?"

"No, not a headache." She met my gaze with a shaky smile. "Everything is just fine."

Her attention fell to the book on the counter. "Is this yours?"

I shook my head. "No. I thought it was yours."

The back door swung open, clattered against the wall, and Ma stumbled in, coughing, her hand over her mouth.

I dropped the napkins on the counter and rushed to her side. "Ma? Are you okay?"

She shook her head and dropped her hand to point toward the back door. Her face was as white as the boxes she packed doughnuts in.

"Ma? Are you sick?"

She swallowed hard as she shook her head again. "No. Yes. Not yet." She took a deep, trembly breath. "Don't go out there!"

I couldn't imagine what was so bad in the trash outside that she'd had this reaction.

She shocked both of us by grasping Abbie's arm then dragging her across the room to the counter where Ma had set her purse. "It's Philip. He's outside on the ground."

She yanked her cell phone from her handbag. The color returned to her face in two tiny red patches on her cheeks. Somehow that was worse than her dead white face. She punched in some numbers.

"Philip? As in Philip Grenville?" A tremor of apprehension wormed up my back.

Ma nodded. "Don't go out there."

Abbie wasn't moving, and Ma released her arm and took a deep breath. "Hello? 911? I need to report a shooting."

Mute and motionless, I listened to Ma bark orders at the dispatcher.

"Yes, he's dead," Ma said into the phone. "Yes, I know who it is." She reached over and clasped Abbie's arm again. "His name is Philip Grenville."

I had the proverbial breath-caught-in-my-throat reaction to that. Abbie's face blanched so white she could have played the part of a vampire in an old horror flick.

I didn't hear the rest of what my mother said because Abbie burst into motion, escaping Ma's grip—not a small feat—and heading for the back door.

"Trish." Ma frantically caught my eye and put her hand over the receiver. "Don't let her see him. I. . .think a hunter shot him. It's. . .bad."

She didn't have to say more. I was already running after Abbie. As she snatched the door open, I grabbed at her arm, but she jerked away from me, almost stumbling down the wooden stairs.

"Abbie. Stop!"

She didn't listen. By the time I caught up with her, she was kneeling in the sparse grass beside Philip's body.

I'd seen dead bodies before. Two to be exact. The first was Jim Bob Jenkins. The second was Georgia Winters, a teacher at the high school. But this was different. Philip was someone I had known well at one time.

Abbie was murmuring Philip's name, pushing at his body. I guess shock shielded her from seeing harsh reality.

I glanced at him. What looked like bruises marred one side of his face. I averted my gaze so I wouldn't see the rest. "Abbie, you shouldn't—"

"Shut up," she snapped. She finally tugged one of his

hands from under his body and put her finger on his wrist.

I couldn't stop her, but I knew checking for vital signs was a waste of time. He was dead.

My stomach roiled, and I was trying desperately to keep my gaze off his inert form. I swallowed hard. I put my hand on Abbie's shoulder. "Come on. You can't do anything for him. We need to wait for help to arrive." And I had to get back inside before I lost control of my stomach.

This time she listened to me. She stood and swayed. I gripped her arm to steady her.

"I just talked to him," she said softly. "Just this afternoon."

My heart skipped. I stared up into her tear-filled eyes. "What?"

She wiped tears from her cheeks and left a streak of Philip's blood on her parchment-white skin. My stomach turned.

"And he came to my book signing at the festival."

"I didn't see him there," I said.

"He came after you left. I wouldn't talk to him." Her voice was getting higher. "He called me this morning. Then he showed up here."

"You never said anything about it. You didn't tell me he was in town."

"I—I told him to get lost." Her nose was running, and I searched my pockets for a tissue but came up empty-handed.

"It was like he was stalking me," she said. "I didn't tell anybody. Not even Eric. I just couldn't tell him. Not yet."

"Oh, Abs. . ." My voice trailed off. She was wrong if she thought nobody knew. Someone always knows. Especially in this town. Unfortunately, the ones who *didn't* know were the people she should have told to begin with.

"What am I going to do?" She hiccuped.

"I don't know." I wouldn't say what I was really thinking—like this wasn't a good way for the detective to find out his fiancée had been in touch with her estranged ex-husband and kept it a secret. Especially so close to their wedding day.

I tugged at Abbie's arm. "Come on. We need to go inside. We've already messed up the crime scene."

"Crime scene?" Her eyes grew wide. "You don't think this was a hunting accident?"

I glanced around. The church was in an isolated location, a no-hunting zone, next to the woods. It *was* hunting season. "Maybe. I guess it could have been." But even as I said the words, I didn't believe them. Something inside me was tingling. I wasn't sure why, but my gut told me this wasn't an accident.

4

Forty minutes later, the building was crawling with deputies, emergency workers, and then the medical examiner guy. I knew the drill. We had all been separated and given an initial interview. I sat in a front room of the church hall with a bored deputy watching over me.

I kept glancing out the window. Unfortunately, the view was of the front parking lot, not the back. I watched vehicles arriving, including several state police cars. I wondered why they were here.

My thoughts were muddled. Questions tumbled one over the other in my head. Like how did Philip get here? There hadn't been any cars in the parking lot when I came.

From the corner of my eye, I saw another sheriff's office car pull up. A familiar Santa Claus–like figure got out. Corporal Nick Fletcher. I had been wishing Eric was here, but the corporal was just as good. He was one of Eric's best friends, as well as a close working companion.

He entered the building, and I hoped he'd come find me. I wasn't disappointed. I heard footsteps outside the room, then the door swung open. He walked in, and I shot to my feet.

He nodded at the deputy, eyes dark under drawn brows and deep furrows in his forehead. "Hey, Mrs. C."

"Corporal Fletcher. I'm so glad you're here."

A brief, warm smile passed over his lips. "Always good to see you, but I have to say, I don't like the circumstances. Better if it was social. Like Abbie and Eric's wedding."

"Isn't that the truth," I said.

He shook his head. "This is bad."

His tight inflection said it all. Anxiety clawed at my brain. "Was Philip shot by accident?"

He and the younger deputy exchanged brief glances before Fletcher answered me. "Any kind of death like this is treated as suspicious until proven otherwise."

"Are you helping with the investigation, then?"

He shook his head. "I'm not here officially. Eric called and asked me to stop by to make sure Abbie was okay."

"I don't understand," I said. "Why aren't you official?"

The deputy behind me stared at the wall.

"You gotta understand, Mrs. C. It's a conflict of interest. The victim is the ex-husband of my superior officer's fiancée. I can't be involved."

"Does that mean Eric can't be involved in the investigation, either?"

"Absolutely not. In fact, they've already brought in the state police."

"The state police? That's why they're here?"

He nodded. "That way, our agency can't be accused of conflict of interest."

"Well, at least Abbie couldn't have done it." I took a deep breath. "Neither could I. We weren't anywhere near here."

I thought he'd look relieved, but he didn't.

"What's wrong?" I asked.

He shifted on his feet, and his belt creaked. "Things aren't always that easily dismissed. They're going to be extra careful not to show favoritism since Abbie is involved and she's Eric's fiancée."

"What does that mean?" I asked.

"She'll be treated fine if things are as they seem, but they can't afford to lose a case due to poor investigation. And the investigation will include looking into the lives of everyone involved. Now I'd better go see what's going on." His lips were set in a grim line. "You gotta stay out of this, Mrs. C. I've had about enough of rescuing you from the hands of murderers."

The deputy opened the door for Corporal Fletcher, who disappeared.

"Do you know how long I'm going to be here?" I asked the deputy.

"No, ma'am," he said.

"I need to make a phone call."

He inhaled and frowned.

The tense atmosphere made me cranky. "I just need to tell my husband where I am so he doesn't worry. Is that okay?"

He sighed. "Yes, ma'am. I need to listen, though."

"That's fine. I don't care who hears." He'd be bored to tears by my conversation, I was sure.

When Max picked up the phone, I heard Chris crying in the background.

"Hi, honey," I said. "Things okay there?" I wasn't sure how to tell him I was once again involved in a crime.

"Yes." He sighed. "I'll be glad when teething is over. Chris is so much louder than Sammie ever was. Although I'm beginning to wonder if this is just his personality. And Charlie's snake escaped. We're still looking for it."

Neither fact surprised me. "I'm sorry, honey. Chris isn't an easy baby. And Charlie is so excited about his new snake, he walks around with it all the time. But then sometimes he puts it down to do something and forgets."

I felt the deputy's gaze on me.

"Hang on, Trish," Max said. I heard the muffled voices of my kids through the receiver. "Honey, I have to go. Will you be home soon?"

"I'm not sure. I have something to tell you." I took a deep breath, worried about Max's reaction to Philip's murder.

"Hang on again," he said. I heard his hand cover the receiver and then his muffled voice. "Charlie! Tell me you did not put your snake in Karen's room." He paused. "Go get it *now*." His hand rustled on the receiver. "Okay, I'm back. Now, what?"

"Um, Max, something bad has happened."

There was a slight pause on his end. "Worse than a missing snake, a teething baby, and an angry teenager?"

"Yes. Much worse."

He inhaled. "What?"

"Philip is dead."

Max didn't say anything for a second. I could almost hear his brain clicking.

"That's Abbie's ex-husband," I said.

"Oh, wow." Max paused. "That's too bad. Was he in an accident?"

"No." I glanced up at the deputy and decided not to say anything more about Abbie.

"What happened?"

I swallowed. "He was, ah, shot. Killed."

"You mean, on the job? He was still a police officer, right?"

"I think he was, but no, it wasn't job related—that I know of."

Max's breath hissed in the receiver. "He was murdered?"

"I don't know."

"You mean, he was in town?" Max asked. "Here?"

The deputy cleared his throat.

"Max, I have to go."

"Wait. Tell me you didn't find the body. Please?"

I picked my nails. "Well, not exactly."

"Not exactly?"

"No." Movement in the parking lot caught my attention. Another police car had arrived. This one unmarked. A woman built like a bulldog stepped from the vehicle. I watched her stride toward the building.

"Where are you?" Max's tone was a mixture of concern and irritation.

"I'm at Ma's church fellowship hall. And no, I didn't find Philip. My mother found him."

"Your mother. . .what? She found him at church?" Chris's wails in the background grew louder.

"Yeah. He was in the back on the pavement behind the church hall."

"Shot?" I heard Charlie's voice in the background and Karen yelling at him. "There's no way you could have been involved, right?" Max asked breathlessly.

My poor husband. He's always having to pick up the pieces when I do something outrageous.

Somebody walked into the room behind me, but I didn't pay attention. "No. No way."

"Good," Max said.

"Mrs. Cunningham, you need to get off the phone," the deputy said. "We need to take you to the sheriff's office for questioning."

My stomach clenched, and I nodded. "Max, I've got to go. They want to question me at the sheriff's office."

"Do you want me to come down there and meet you?"

"No. I'm fine." I stood to follow the deputy. I could just imagine Max in the foyer of the sheriff's office with a screaming baby, Sammie, Charlie, and a snake.

"All right, baby. Call me as soon as you can. I love you."

"Okay, and I love you, too." I hung up and stuck the phone in my pocket.

~

Quite awhile later, at the sheriff's office, a deputy walked me to an interview room. Having been involved with two other murder investigations, I knew the drill. But the bad thing was, I'd finally gotten used to Detective Eric Scott, and he wasn't here. I was going to have to deal with someone new.

I waited for a few minutes, biting my nails, wondering where Abbie was. Then the woman I'd seen exiting her car at the church hall rolled into the room like a Mack truck, shutting the door behind her. She carried Abbie's book in a plastic bag.

The skin on her face had seen more sun than moisturizer or makeup. I imagined she intimidated most people with her size and her attitude. When I meet someone with a chip on their shoulder, I always want to knock it off, and hers was so large, it would be a fun challenge.

I had a sudden, vivid memory from high school, when I rumbled with a girl who reminded me of this woman. She had insulted Abbie, who was shy and wouldn't stand up for herself. Although bruised and a little bloody, I'd prevailed in the fight, despite our differences in size, much to my delight and my parents' chagrin.

Given that I felt the same way about the woman standing in front of me right now, I could tell the Lord still had a lot of stuff to work out of me.

"Mrs. Cunningham?"

I stared up at her. "Yes?"

"Thank you for waiting for me. I'm Detective Reid with the state police. We're temporarily using the sheriff's office for interviews."

"You're welcome." *Like I had a choice?* My antenna was up. Her eyes were flat and unemotional, and she eyed me like a praying mantis would size up its prey. She was a force to be reckoned with.

She yanked out a chair and sat down. Then she pulled out a notebook and pen from her pocket. She ran the tip of the pen slowly down several pages, as though reading her notes. I knew she was faking.

"So, Mrs. Cunningham." She glanced up quickly. "Did you know the deceased?"

"Yes, I did."

She stared at me. "How did you know him?'

"He is. . .was. . .the ex-husband of my best friend, Abbie Grenville."

"Uh-huh." She ran her pen down the list again. Then stared at me from eyes untouched by makeup. "How well did you know him?"

I shrugged. "I hadn't seen him in years. So—not well anymore, I guess."

"Years," she repeated. "So that means you haven't seen him lately?"

"Yes. That's what that means." I wished with all my heart that Eric would walk into the room and take over the questioning.

"Were you aware of his recent whereabouts?"

"If by that you mean, was I aware that he was in town? yes. But I hadn't seen him."

She continued her interrogation, asking me detailed questions about my steps from the time I arrived at the church to the time the first deputy came on the scene. I had to describe Philip's body and what Abbie had done when we were outside.

When I was done with my recitation, she inhaled and exhaled slowly and then dangled Abbie's novel in the plastic bag in front of my eyes. "Is this yours?"

"No," I said. "It isn't."

It wasn't Abbie's. It wasn't mine. It wasn't my mother's. Whose was it? I wondered if the detective was going to read it. If so, it wasn't going to look good for Abbie. An ex-spouse shooting an ex-spouse?

"What time did you arrive at the church hall?" she snapped.

"Around four," I said.

"When you arrived, was Abbie Grenville there?"

"No," I said.

"When did she arrive?"

"About fifteen minutes after my mom and I got there."

I met Detective Reid's cold, watchful gaze. "And had she been there earlier?"

"Yes," I said. My thoughts dropped in line like playing cards in a game of solitaire. Of course Abbie had been there earlier. That meant she theoretically could have killed Philip.

The detective stood. "Thank you. That will be all."

5

When I was finally driven back to my car in the church fellowship hall parking lot, it was dark. I was shaking. I'd been interviewed before—after both murder investigations I was involved in—but Eric was a whole different kind of person than Detective Reid. He at least had an innate kindness. She seemed to have no soul.

My mother had called my cell and left me a message that she was headed home after her interview at the sheriff's office to make dinner and that she'd called Max and invited him. He'd accepted, to my relief. I needed to be around my family. All of them.

Abbie's car was still in the parking lot. That wasn't good news. Inside my SUV, I called Eric's cell phone and left a message for him. Then I tried to reach Abbie, but she didn't answer.

As I drove to my folks' house, my mind continued to turn questions over again and again so rapidly, I felt nauseated. What had Philip been doing back in town? And why had he been trying to talk to Abbie? Why was he at the church? What time had he been shot? Was it murder or an accident? And, the very worst thought, was Abbie a suspect?

When I pulled up to the farm, Max wasn't there yet. Daddy was walking from the barn to the house illuminated by the lights he'd installed on the outbuildings. He met me and pulled me into a bear hug as soon as I got out of my vehicle. My purse banged against our legs. "Sugar bug, you managed to get involved in trouble again."

I snuggled against him, feeling his warmth against the cold fall air. "Not me this time, Daddy," I said into his shoulder. "Ma found Philip. And it's Abbie I'm worried about."

He sighed. The scent of the outside lingered in his heavy coat, reminding me of childhood and safety and good things. How I wished right now that Abbie and I were still kids and she was visiting me. We'd go running up to my bedroom to share secrets. And we'd be ignorant of what it was like to be adults.

"I'm praying for her," Daddy said. "Your mother was pretty upset—and not just about finding Philip. She overheard someone say something about evidence pointing at Abbie." He backed up and took my chin in his hand. "Sugar bug, we've all got good reason to be upset. There's something you should know."

I frowned up at him.

"And if the police ask me, I'll have to tell the truth."

I felt my breath come faster. "What is it?"

He took a deep breath. "When Abbie was writing her book, she asked me to help her learn about guns. Remember?"

I nodded.

"Well, I helped her learn to shoot a thirty-aught-six."

I thought about Daddy's rifles, which he kept in a cabinet in the barn. "That's your favorite hunting rifle, and. . ." I realized where he was going. "That's the kind of gun she used in her book." I felt my voice growing shrill. "I don't know what Philip was shot with."

Daddy rubbed my arms. "Hopefully it wasn't a rifle

like that. And maybe no one will ask me about it. But I think I'm in the acknowledgments of her book."

My earlier anxiety gripped me like a vise. "I have to try to reach Eric again." I pulled away from Daddy and reached into my purse.

Daddy patted my arm. "Trish, you've got to remember that God is in control."

"Right."

I wondered if he heard the sarcasm in my voice. Daddy said nothing, just patted me one more time then headed for the house, which was good, because I didn't want him to know my momentary angry thoughts. Like why had God allowed this to happen? Abbie finally had a chance to be happy with a new man, and along comes her ex-husband to ruin her life again by getting killed. Not that he'd done it on purpose.

I forced myself to breathe deeply while I punched in Eric's number. This time he answered.

"Trish? Is Abbie okay? I haven't been able to reach her. Tell me what's happened."

"Didn't Corporal Fletcher tell you?" I asked.

"Yes, but I want to hear it from you."

His voice had a desperate edge that made me shiver in the cold air. I forced my voice to remain calm. "Ma found Philip dead behind the church hall. Abbie and I were there. We were all taken to the sheriff's office for questioning by a bulldog state police detective."

"Reid," he said.

"Yep. You know her?"

"*Of* her," he said. "So what happened exactly?"

I explained everything. "And I'm really worried about Abbie. . . ."

"Why, exactly?" he asked.

"Because she moved the body to check his pulse. And because of the book on the counter that didn't belong to her or me or Ma—"

"Whose book was it? Do you know?"

"I have no idea, but, Eric. . .she could have done it. She was there alone before Ma and I got there. And you know what her latest book is about, don't you?"

I heard him groan.

"Eric, Abbie told me that—"

"Stop," he snapped. "Don't tell me anything she said to you. If I know and it's something they haven't discovered yet, I'll have to tell them. And I can't deal with all of this from out here. I'll be home tomorrow. I'll see her then."

"Yes. Okay." The awkward position Eric was in finally hit me. Torn between two worlds. His occupation and his fiancée. His job was to support the men and women investigating this case, even at the expense of people's comfort. But he wanted more than anything to protect Abbie. How could he do both?

He made me promise to get in touch with him if anything else happened. He also requested that I watch over Abbie—something both of us knew he didn't have to ask.

As I put my phone in my pocket, I realized I hadn't seen Buddy, my father's dog. Usually he'd have greeted me with enthusiasm. I wondered where he was. I shivered again, but before I could head for the house and warmth, Max and the kids arrived.

I waited. Charlie and Sammie scrambled from the car, and Karen took Chris from his car seat and followed more slowly. They all greeted me with a chorus of "Hi, Mom" and went inside.

When Max got out, I threw myself into his arms like Sammie does. The problem is, I'm not as small as our daughter, so Max fell back against the car.

"Hey, hey," he said when he'd regained his balance. He wrapped his arms around me and kissed the top of my head. Then he lifted my chin and made me meet his gaze.

"So how are you? Okay? You survived questioning?"

"Yes. They had to turn everything over to the state police since Abbie is engaged to Eric."

"That doesn't surprise me," he said. "How is she?"

"I haven't talked to her since they separated us at the fellowship hall." I took his arm, and we walked toward the house.

"Did you tell the kids?" I asked.

"I said something to Karen but not to the little kids." He shook his head. "I wanted to wait until we knew more details. I'm not sure how much they really need to know."

"Good," I said. "I'm really worried about Abbie."

He glanced down at me. "Why?"

"They were questioning her at the sheriff's office, and that detective woman is awful." I gave him the abbreviated version as we stepped through the back door and into the mudroom. There we shucked off our coats and headed into the kitchen, where my mother was working.

The steamy, warm, delicious-smelling air seemed completely at odds with the icy worry that had wrapped itself around my heart.

"This sounds pretty serious for Abbie," Max said when I was finished.

"Oh, it's serious," my mother piped up. She was cooking a spread worthy of Thanksgiving and Christmas combined. Her solution for any kind of calamity is food and lots of it.

Max glanced from her to me. "I can get Abbie a lawyer if she needs one." He knows lots of great lawyers. Tough, Harvard-educated lawyers.

I felt a sense of relief. "Thank you, honey."

He kissed me again and then greeted Ma with a kiss on her cheek.

Daddy walked into the kitchen, followed by Charlie and Sammie. "Hello, Max."

"Simon," Max said and gripped Daddy in a quick guy hug.

Sammie rushed Max and grabbed him around the hips. "We're going out to look at some new calves. Wanna come?"

"You bet," Max said. Then he turned to me. "You gonna be okay, baby?"

I waved him on. "Yep. You go. I need to help Ma here."

Charlie chased Sammie out to the mudroom where they pulled on their coats. I heard Chris in the other room where Karen was watching television. Daddy and Max followed more slowly, putting on their outer garments.

"Have you talked to Abbie?" Ma asked as soon as the back door was shut.

"No. I can't reach her. I'm really worried. Especially since I talked to Eric and Corporal Fletcher. Both of them sound worried." I explained to her what they had said to me.

Ma sighed.

"So you're sure he was murdered, and you think they suspect her?" I asked.

"Yes. Especially the way they took her out of there.

And then you know they found Philip's car just up the road."

"They did? Why didn't we see it?"

"The other direction. None of us passed it on the way to the hall."

"How do you know this?" I asked.

"I overheard them talking in another room." Ma smiled for the first time since I'd arrived. "People assume since I have gray hair I can't hear."

Assuming anything about my mother is a mistake. And it was my opinion that her hearing was finely tuned by daily practice at the shop. How else would she be able to pick up the choice bits of gossip she did, if she didn't have the hearing of a bat?

She pointed at the refrigerator. "Slice the ham that's in there." She worked at the counter with hard motions, but she glanced at me from the corner of her eye. "You need to solve this mystery. You have to help Abbie."

"I gave up solving mysteries, Ma. You know that. Last time was too much. I almost got killed, and Chris would have been killed with me. It's not worth it."

"You can do it and be safe. God will protect you. Don't you care about your best friend?"

I thought it was a little presumptuous to assume God would automatically protect me, especially when I hadn't even prayed about it yet.

Ma was making chicken. In addition to the ham.

"Fried chicken *and* ham?" I asked. "It's like a holiday or something."

Ma's hand hit the counter with a thud, and she stood still, looking out the kitchen window where Daddy, Max,

Sammie, and Charlie stood at the fence watching the new calves in the field. "Sometimes it's good to just celebrate being alive."

I'm so used to fending off my mother's sarcastic comments and odd ideas that when she says something profound, I'm speechless. I walked over and hugged her shoulders.

She patted my hands. "You've got to help Abbie." Her tone was unusually soft. "I don't want to see her wedding postponed. I have a feeling about this, and it's not good."

Ma's insistence tore at my resolve. "I promise I'll think about it." I went back to slicing ham.

"I'll help," Ma said. "I can collect information, too."

I glanced at her with horror. "Ma, no—"

"Don't argue with me." She faced me with blazing eyes. "Abbie is like a daughter to us. And she's like a sister to you. Family. Maybe not by blood, but in our hearts."

I put my hands up in surrender. "You're right, Ma. She *is* family. I just don't want anyone to be hurt. . .any more than they have been already."

Her body deflated. "Don't think I'm insensitive to how you feel."

I wasn't sure what she meant. Besides, sensitivity wasn't one of my mother's strong points, so I had my doubts. But she was in an unusual mood tonight, and I was seeing a side of her I rarely glimpsed.

Her shoulders drooped. "I never thought before how it felt to find a dead person," she said. "Now I know."

I swallowed. "It is awful. It's the shock of seeing the shell of a person. Knowing they were there but are now gone."

"Exactly." She sniffed and straightened.

I knew that in a weird way, she was apologizing to me for not understanding the other times I'd been involved in murder. I was grateful.

"Well, gracious." Ma rinsed off her hands and went back to work on the chicken. "This dinner isn't going to put itself on the table. Let's get to work."

~

Later, when we were all seated at the dining room table, the blessing said and the food passed, Ma glanced at me. "In all the. . .confusion today, I forgot. Jaylene came by the shop and told me you bought some things for a cat?"

Sammie bounced in her chair. "I'm getting a kitten. Grandmother Cunningham is buying it for me."

"What?" My mother stared at me. "I didn't know about this. Trish? You aren't that fond of cats—especially inside."

"I know, but. . ."

"You let that woman—"

"I think it's wonderful that Trish is doing this for Sammie," Daddy said before Ma could finish her thought.

I met Max's glance, and he winked at me. He knows how my mother feels about his mother, but she usually wasn't so vocal in front of the children.

Ma realized what she'd almost done and had the grace to blush. "Well now, I suppose that's a good thing. After all, Charlie's got his snake."

"After months of nagging," I said.

Karen glared at her little brother. "He purposefully

put the snake in my bed today."

"I can't help it that he fell off my shoulder," Charlie said.

Karen glared at him. "Well, I hope Sammie's cat eats your snake."

Sammie's eyes grew huge. "No! That's not nice at all."

"Karen," Max said. "Don't start, please."

Karen and Charlie were always like water and oil. He knew just how to push her buttons to get her to react.

The normalcy of their bantering helped me to relax, although I was forcing myself to eat because I knew I needed to, despite my stomach's protests. I felt Max's gaze and looked up at him.

I love you, he mouthed.

We all ate in silence for a while, and then Ma put her fork down. "Well, did your daddy tell you that Buddy took sick last week? Vet says he's not doing well. He mostly stays in the barn now. And we let him sleep in the house at night."

That explained why Buddy hadn't greeted me when I arrived.

"Gotta get another dog, I guess," Daddy said. "I should do it before Buddy. . ." His voice trailed off.

"Does that mean he's going to die?" Charlie never missed a thing.

"Yes," Ma said. "And he'll go to doggy heaven. Now would anyone like more mashed potatoes?"

I met Daddy's gaze. He smiled at me, but his eyes were watering. He and Buddy were inseparable. I felt tears well up in my own eyes.

He saw them and reached across the table and patted my hand. "Buddy lived a good long life. It's the cycle of things, sugar bug. You know that. For everything there is a season. A time to be born and a time to die."

"I know." I swallowed and thought about that. Buddy was old for a dog. And though it was sad, he'd lived out his full years. But what about Philip? His life had been cut short. Even though I hadn't liked him for what he did to Abbie, I never would have wished him dead in a pool of blood on the ground.

After the kids left the table, the four adults sat and drank decaf coffee, pretending everything was normal. Max talked about Tommy at college. But my mind wasn't in what anyone was saying. I kept thinking about Abbie.

"You know what's weird?" I said during a lull in the conversation. "Jaylene said Henry knew that Philip was back in town. She was pretty nasty about Philip."

"Doesn't surprise me none," Ma said. "The Adlers hated him."

I glanced at her, surprised. "Why?"

Ma shrugged. "Not really sure, but you can start your investigation by talking to Jaylene."

From the corner of my eye, I saw Max's head swivel toward me. I didn't look at him, but I knew I'd hear about this later. Max didn't want me to investigate any more than I wanted to.

"We can get this done fast," Ma said. "That detective isn't nearly as smart as she'd like to think. You wouldn't believe the questions she asked me."

Unfortunately, I thought the bulldog was a lot smarter than Ma gave her credit for. I just hoped she was smart enough to see that Abbie wasn't guilty of murder.

Had I decided to do it? I didn't want to do it. I

wanted to pretend everything was okay and just let the police handle it. I thought about everything Ma had said. Abbie was my best friend. Closer than a sister. Did I have a choice?

After a terse "We have to talk," Max took the kids home so I could stop by Abbie's apartment in town. She still wasn't answering her phone. Ma sent several plates of food along with me, despite my arguments that Abbie wouldn't be eating. When I pulled up, her car was there, parked along the street. She lived above a shop in downtown Four Oaks.

I sat in my SUV for a moment, gathering my emotions. Abbie and I were opposites. I was a fiery volcano. She was an icy mountain spring. She always held her counsel, maintaining rigid control of herself and everything in her life, even when she was falling apart inside. I tended to fly off all over the place. To act and speak before I thought.

But now I needed to temper myself. Be confident and strong for her and watch my tongue, even though I felt like coming apart.

Balancing my load of food, I walked up the stairs to her apartment and banged on her door.

"Abbie, I know you're in there. I'll use my key if you don't answer."

I heard her steps coming to the door, then the lock turning.

I expected her to look bad, but I tried not to gasp at her appearance. Abbie rarely let herself be seen without being perfectly made up. Mascara ran in dark trails from her bloodshot eyes down her white cheeks. The only other color on her face was her red nose and eyes. She motioned me in, turned, and walked to the couch, where she dropped into a corner and pulled a blanket around her shoulders. Only one lamp was on in the room. A small, decorative brass thing that only served to prove how dark the rest of the apartment was.

I held up the plates that my mother had sent. "Ma sent food. Do you want something?"

"I would throw up," she said.

"That's what I told Ma." I turned on another light so I wouldn't fall over anything. Abbie blinked but didn't complain. She had a half-empty box of tissues next to her. The coffee table was littered with wadded, used tissues, but there was no sign of any kind of nourishment.

"I'll put this away. And I'm making you some tea. Don't argue." I took the food to the kitchen and put it in the refrigerator. Then I put water in the teakettle and set it on the range.

While I waited, I straightened things up. The kitchen was as big a mess as Abbie. Another indication she was falling apart.

After the tea was made, I carried two cups to the living room, along with a trash bag. After putting the cups on the coffee table, I turned on another light. Then I gathered up all the used tissues. "This won't do, you know," I said. "You can't sit here in the dark. You can't let them get to you."

I heard sniffling and turned to look at her. She was crying. "I—I just talked to June. Philip's mother."

"Oh, Abs. . ." I sat next to her and hugged her. "That's brave of you."

I felt her tears wet on my cheek and her body shaking.

My tall, cool friend was trembling.

"They think I did it," she said. "That detective was so hostile. She questioned me for hours. So invasive. I feel violated. And I just wanted to tell June that I didn't kill him."

"Did she believe you?" I asked. I knew the two women had been in contact over the years.

"Yes." Abbie sniffed. "I think so."

"Good." I held her more tightly, and for once, she let me. "I can't even imagine how you feel. I'm so sorry. Have you talked to Eric?"

She hiccuped. "Yes, just for a minute. I told him I didn't want to discuss things until he returns. This is a nightmare."

I agreed, but I didn't say that. I finally let her go and handed her a cup of tea. "Drink this."

She wanted to refuse, but I just glared at her. After a brief battle of wills, she took the cup.

"Max can find you a good lawyer," I said.

Abbie's lips trembled. "I don't want to have to have a lawyer. When a suspect *lawyers up*, the cops see it as suspicious behavior."

I shook my head. "They're already looking at you with suspicion, remember?"

She swallowed. "It's worse than you think," she whispered. Tears filled her eyes again, and her nose started running.

"Blow your nose and then tell me why."

She obeyed and then took several deep, halting breaths. "I don't know if I can."

"Spit it out," I said.

"Philip was there with me at the church. Maybe even

right before he was killed."

My vision seemed to go black, and I could only see Abbie through a tiny pinpoint. "With you?"

She nodded and started crying again. "That was the third time I'd seen him."

My chest constricted.

"The first time was at my book signing at the festival. I was so mad that he was there. I wouldn't talk to him, and he finally left. In a big hurry. Today he ran into me at the Gas 'n' Go. We argued. I—I was very angry. I left him there. After I arrived at the church, he showed up. That's why I left and went to McDonald's."

"How did he know you were at the church? Did you tell him you were going there?"

She shook her head. "But the police know we were at the store together. They found a receipt in his pocket from the Gas 'n' Go, so they went out there and looked at the security tapes. Our argument is there to see." Her mouth twisted. "The thing is, I never saw him buy anything. But maybe he did after I left."

I was having trouble breathing. She picked up her tea but was trembling too hard to drink any, so she put the cup back down.

"Remember how manipulative he used to be?" she asked. "How he always made me feel like he was right and I was wrong?"

"Yes. That used to make me feel so horrible for you." I closed my eyes then opened them again. "There's no way they can say you did it, right? His shooting wasn't close and personal."

She clasped her hands so tightly, her knuckles were

white. "Yes, they could say I did it. I was angry. I locked the door and left him standing in the front parking lot. He could have walked around back. There's a road that skims around the church property. They could say I might have driven up there, stopped the car, and shot him."

"With what?"

"My hunting rifle."

I know my mouth fell open. "You have a hunting rifle?"

"Had," she said. "I had one."

"When?"

"When my grandmother died and left me everything, there were some guns in her stuff that had belonged to some of the men in her family."

"Do you have them now?"

"No. I gave them to Philip when we were married. But they were listed in her will, and I was the sole beneficiary. And now he's dead. With a shot from a rifle. What if it's like one that I had?"

"How would the cops know that? Tell me you didn't tell them?"

She closed her eyes and then opened them again. "Do you have any idea what that kind of interrogation is like? I didn't. Even though I know cops. I've never been on that side of the table. By the time she was done with me, I was ready to admit anything just to be able to leave." Fresh tears dripped down her face. "I'm so stupid."

"I think you mean naive." I leaned over and hugged her again then sat back. "So did Philip have his car with him?"

"Yeah," she said. "A blue Honda."

"Remember, there was no Honda in the parking lot when we were in the hall right before Ma found him."

Her eyes grew wide. "I didn't even think about that. Where was his car?"

"Down the road. Ma overheard the deputies talking about it."

"That's weird," Abbie said.

I nodded. "Yes, it is. And did he have a copy of your book with him when you saw him?"

She shook her head. "No. That's weird, too. I don't know where that book came from."

I thought it was strange, too. "Hey, I talked to Eric tonight. He said he's coming home tomorrow."

"Yeah." She stared at me with glazed eyes. "I think we need to postpone the wedding. He disagrees."

"I do, too," I said. "We all finally convinced you to get married, and now you're talking about postponing it?"

A tremulous grin crossed her lips; then it died, and she started crying again. "Trish, I can't get married in a jail cell."

"You aren't going to jail." I sat up straight. I knew without a doubt what I had to do. "I'm going to solve this mystery. I refuse to let them take you down."

For a moment, I saw a glint of hope in her eyes. Then she blinked and shook her head violently. "No. I can't let you. It's too dangerous."

"You can't stop me." I stood and went over to her desk and started rummaging for some paper and a pencil.

"What are you doing?" she asked.

"I'm going to take notes. And when I get home, I'm going to transfer them to a steno pad." I whirled around to face her and waved the pen at her like a baton. "Start talking, Abbie. I want to know everything you can possibly remember."

When I got home, Max met me in the kitchen.

I dropped my purse on the table, feeling like I was a hundred years old. His expression was a mixture of concern and determination.

I wanted to avoid the discussion I knew we were gong to have. "How are the kids?"

"Karen is giving Chris a bath. Charlie is doing some homework. And Sammie is doing some kind of project in her room."

"Good."

"How is Abbie?" He began rubbing my shoulders. His way of softening me up before telling me he didn't want me to investigate.

But his tender touch got to me, and the tough shell I'd portrayed to Abbie began to crack under his attention. I bit my lip trying to keep myself from blubbering.

"Honey?" He turned me around and stared into my eyes.

"Abbie's not good. Not at all." I disengaged myself from his grasp and went to the sink for a glass of water, just to have something to do so I wouldn't fall apart. "I'm sorry you had to deal with the kids all evening. I know you have a lot going on. I'm just. . ."

"It's fine. Really. I'm so sorry about Abbie. The timing is terrible."

"Yes, it is." I filled a glass, took a sip, and stared at the dark night through the window. "She's talking about calling off the wedding." Tears filled my eyes, and I couldn't see. "The bad thing is, she might have to."

"I can see why she'd say that," he said. "The investigation might go on for a while."

I whirled around. "Yes. I know that. But it's worse than just that. Things don't look good for her because she could have shot Philip." The pitch of my voice kept rising. "He was there with her at the church. Alone."

Shock rippled across his face. "Whew."

"Yeah, whew," I said.

"I'm serious about helping her find a good lawyer." He leaned his hip against the counter. "I'm sorry to say this, but she might need one, given that fact. I'm sorry, baby." He paused and studied me. "You're not going to get involved. Right?"

I took a deep breath, stepped toward him, and met his gaze with my chin in the air. "Yes, I am. I'm going to at least try to solve this mystery."

His nostrils flared. "I was hoping I'd misunderstood things at your mother's. I thought you'd had it with solving mysteries."

"I have—last time scared me so bad. But this is Abbie we're talking about."

He crossed his arms. "I don't like it. Let the police do their job."

"You're the one who just said it sounded like she might actually need that lawyer. I've got to find out what happened. That detective is. . .well, awful."

He ran his fingers through his hair. "It terrifies me." After he took a couple of deep breaths, he shook his head. "No. I can't agree to it. I just have a feeling about this."

I did, too, and it scared me. I blinked back tears, turned away from him, and leaned my forehead against the cool metal of the refrigerator. "You didn't see her, Max. You know how Abbie is. Tall. Cool. Always perfect. She was crumpled up in a ball in the corner of her couch." I started to cry. "That detective ripped her to shreds."

I heard his steps cross the kitchen floor, and he wrapped his arms around me. I leaned back against his chest.

"What if his murder had nothing to do with anyone around here?" Max asked. "What if it had to do with his job? Some kind of drug dealer or something. What then?"

"Then it will be obvious real soon, won't it?" I pulled away from his grasp and turned around. "The killer would have to be a stranger. How many strangers come into town unnoticed? I could find that out easily enough."

"That wasn't my point, and you know it," he said.

"I know what your point was. It could be dangerous. But. . .Abbie." I leaned hard into his chest, smashing my nose flat. "I can't let it go. Please, Max, you have to understand." My voice was muffled.

"So you're just going to collect clues?" he asked softly. "In a notebook."

"Yes." I pulled away from him and looked up into his face. "Wouldn't you do whatever you could to help someone you loved?"

"Yes, but I would also do anything I could to *protect* someone I love."

I knew he was referring to me, but I also knew I'd won my point.

We stood in silence for several moments. The tick-tocks of the grandfather clock in the living room echoed down the hall, reminding me of the passing of time. The short amount of time before Abbie's wedding.

"I can't stop you," Max said finally. "I'm not going to try, because it'll be pointless. Because we'll fight, you'll feel guilty, and I'll feel mean. Just please be careful. And. . .I know you will. . .but please keep the kids out of it."

"Yes. Yes, I will." I totally understood his concern, and for once, I wasn't even offended that he would make a comment like that or imply that I was stupid. "I'll hire a babysitter for Chris and work only when the kids are in school."

Our eyes met, and he gave me a slight grin. "You're incorrigible."

I rubbed my hands up and down his arms. "I'm trying to grow up. Trying to be more careful."

"I know," he said.

"I don't want to talk anymore about this tonight." I heard my youngest begin to cry upstairs, followed by Karen's voice and Charlie's yell to cut out the noise. "I'll go take care of him. See the kids to bed. Take a long, hot bath." I twined my arms around Max's neck and hugged him hard. "Then I want to lie in bed next to you. I want you to hold me tight, and I want to forget about everything."

On Wednesday morning, after I saw the kids off to school and got Chris settled in his playpen, I called Abbie to make sure she was okay. She assured me she was fine, but I knew she was lying. That just gave me more incentive to get to work.

I hadn't slept well, so I made an extrastrong pot of coffee. Then, I took one of my new steno pads from the kitchen drawer and reached in my purse for the notes I'd taken at Abbie's the night before. I stared at my scrawls and felt overwhelmed. I had no clear suspects. No idea where to start. Well, truth be told, there *was* one clear suspect. Abbie. And if I were really honest with myself, in Detective Reid's place, I would be looking hard at her, too. But unlike the detective, I had the advantage of knowing Abbie. And I knew for certain that she hadn't killed Philip.

I tapped my pen on the table and considered my tendency to jump into things without thinking about the consequences. I'd paid dearly for that impulsiveness repeatedly throughout my life. Until this year, the staff at the emergency room knew me by name because of all the times I had thoughtlessly participated in activities that led to some mishap. Like skateboarding with Tommy and his friends at the park, even though I hadn't skateboarded since I was a kid.

But this past year, since my last pregnancy, a sense of my own mortality had finally penetrated my dense brain.

And even more important than that was the realization that I wasn't an island. I needed to consider the consequences of my own actions in the lives of others, particularly those I loved most and who depended on me.

Looking back at the last two mysteries I'd been involved in, I knew I had been impulsive. And I wondered if I'd really given my investigations to the Lord.

However, that wasn't relevant. What mattered was here and now. This time I would. I had to. I couldn't do this on my own. And this time, the circumstances were even more pressing. At best, Abbie might have to postpone her wedding. At worst, she could be thrown in jail.

I bowed my head and asked for guidance. Then I asked God to have mercy on my best friend.

When I was done, I flipped open the steno pad. One key to finding a murderer is knowing the steps that the victim took minutes, hours, and weeks before his or her death. Philip was pretty much an unknown to me. I hadn't seen him in years. And I'd had no idea he was back in town until Jaylene had mentioned him.

I'd have to begin with what Abbie told me and build on that.

I titled the entry "Philip's Actions." Then I wrote what I knew about Philip.

> Philip showed up at Abbie's book signing at the fall festival the weekend before. She refused to talk to him, and he left abruptly. Why?
>
> He caught up with her again at the Gas 'n' Go on the day he was murdered. How did he know she was there? Was he following her? Or was it a coincidence?

She refused to talk to him. They fought. He left. The he went to the church. How did he know she was at the church?

She didn't want to talk to him, so she left and went to McDonald's.

I needed to begin a list of questions I had to answer, so I wrote:

Why was Philip's car parked down the road?

What did Philip want to talk to Abbie about?

Where did Abbie's novel come from, and why was it at the church?

Why did he leave the fall festival so quickly? Because he was mad like he used to get at her?

How did he know she was at the Gas 'n' Go and the church the day he was killed? Was he following Abbie? Or coincidence?

Why was he back in town?

When I'd investigated the two other murders, the suspects had all been present and accounted for at the time. This time, I had no clear suspects. And no obvious reasons that I knew of why someone would kill a man who hadn't been in town in years.

The only people on the scene had been me, Ma, and Abbie. And none of us had done it. I tapped the pen on my chin. Linda had been out there, but did she even know Philip?

To Detective Reid, it might appear that Abbie had good motivation. Philip suddenly returned after years, right before her marriage to Eric, who was an old friend and work buddy of Philip's. But aside from his presence disrupting her life, what good reason would she have to shoot him now?

Then there was Abbie herself. She sometimes holds bits of information back. And I often didn't know what she was really thinking about a certain situation, incident, or person until long after the fact. She was trying to change, but a situation like this might make her retreat again. I couldn't depend on the fact that she was telling me everything. I would have to question her again.

The thing that scared me to death was that she had been in the right place at the right time to kill Philip. She had owned a rifle and was an experienced shot, thanks to my father. And then there was her recently published book. The one about a man who shoots his ex-wife and almost gets away with it.

I tapped my pen against my teeth. How could I approach this?

Trying to approach the mystery by looking for rifle owners wouldn't get me anywhere. We lived in a rural area where most households had rifles because so many people hunted.

I wondered about Max's statement that maybe the murderer was someone Philip had dealt with as a cop. Someone who had followed him here from New York. That was a possibility.

And what about Philip's behavior? That was the most puzzling thing of all. He seemed to have been almost stalking Abbie. Why now? After all these years?

I knew of only two people besides Abbie who were

angry with Philip. The Adlers. I'd start at the Pet Emporium. I'd buy another Kitty Koller. Then I'd stop by Ma's shop. I never knew what kinds of clues I'd pick up there.

I also wanted to talk to Eric. In person, preferably. I glanced at my watch. He would be at work now. I grabbed my cell and dialed, thinking of all my arguments to get him to agree to see me. Eric answered on the second ring.

"Trish, I was going to call you. Can you come to my office? I want to talk."

Well, that was easy. "I was just going to ask you if I could do that."

"Good," he said.

We agreed on a time and hung up. I took a deep breath. There was one other thing I had to do even though it made me feel sick. I needed to go back to the murder scene. I probably wouldn't find anything, but it might help jog something in my head. That meant I had to get a key to the church hall from my mother. And I had to find out when the police would be finished with the scene. Maybe Eric would be able to tell me.

I put the pen down, slapped my notebook shut, tucked it into my purse, and stood. The first thing was to find a babysitter for Chris.

I was counting down to Abbie's wedding. I intended to see that everything went as planned.

After a quick call to Ma for babysitter advice, which she gave me only if I promised to stop by the shop, I decided on Gladys, who went to church with my mother and had lived in a house across the street from my folks' farm since I was a kid. She watched her great-grandchildren on a regular basis, so I wasn't putting her out. She was perfect.

Gladys's house smelled like laundry detergent and cinnamon. A strange but very appealing combination. She had a round face that matched her round waist. When I was little, I visited her often, and she'd ply me with chocolate chip cookies by the dozen and homemade root beer by the gallon.

"Well now, Trish, you just come right on in here. And here's that adorable little boy your mama's brought by." She reached out and took Chris right from my arms. He beamed at her.

"Can I get you somethin' to drink?"

"No, thank you." I was eager to begin my clue collecting.

"Your mama told me you're going to solve this dreadful crime. Someone like Philip Grenville wasn't the kind of person you'd want your daughter to marry, but nobody deserves to die that young and in such a tragic way."

I agreed wholeheartedly. "I don't know where to start."

"Well, your mama says you're the best sleuth around, so I'm sure you can do it."

"I'm not sure I agree with that." I wished my mother would keep her mouth shut about my investigating. "I don't even know how to start this time."

"Well, you just need to clear your head." I followed her into the family room, where she put Chris on the carpeted floor next to a baby very near his age. Then she turned to me. "You know what I think?"

I shook my head, knowing she was about to tell me.

"You need to look at people without moral values. Or

people who are strangers in town."

I wanted to ask her how I could determine whether people had moral values, given that some of the worst killers in history seemed like the salt of the earth. However, her idea about strangers in town was one that I needed to examine. "Do you have any suggestions? Do you know of anyone who has been in town recently who doesn't live here?"

Gladys pursed her lips and *tsk*ed. Then she planted herself on a brown, suedelike sofa. "Why, yes, I do. The good-looking boy. The one everyone fawns over, including two of my granddaughters." Gladys *tsk-tsk*ed again. "Why, even your mother goes googly-eyed. I've never seen Doris have no sense like that before."

There was only one man who fit that bill. "Do you mean Clark? The WWPS delivery guy?"

"That's the one."

"Well, why? He's just a delivery guy. What in the world would he have in common with Philip?"

She snorted. "He's just too good-looking for his own good. He was a model, you know. In New York. Still goes up there a couple times a month."

That explained the fact that he knew he looked good. "I've never seen his picture anywhere," I said.

"Well, of course you haven't. My lands, Trish. You wouldn't read those kinds of magazines."

"What. . ."

Gladys raised an eyebrow.

"Oh," I said. I didn't bother to ask how *she* knew. "Does my mother know?"

Gladys shrugged. "Your mother is too smitten by him. She refuses to believe it."

That was odd, but then, Ma was unpredictable. This was an interesting fact. Philip was from New York. Clark was from New York. "Why is he here? Do you know?"

She shook her head. "Something about his mama, I think. Philip moved her to a nice trailer on the other side of Brownsville. You know. . .in the next county."

I remembered Clark had said something about his mother being sick. This was more and more interesting. I needed to get that autographed bookplate for her and deliver it personally.

"Models do drugs and. . .do other things for money," Gladys said. "I see it enough on the news. Like all those actors and actresses."

I nodded as if in agreement, but I didn't like to make blanket assumptions like that.

"Mark it down," she said. "There's something funny with him. It's not right for a man to do *that* kind of thing. Modeling, indeed."

I left "do *that* kind of thing" alone and said my good-byes. Chris didn't even look up when I walked out the door. I may have found the person I could leave Chris with when I started working with Max. And I'd made up my mind about that. Once I solved this mystery and got Abbie married off, I was determined to work at Cunningham and Son.

I walked into Adler's Pet Emporium. No one was behind the counter, and I yelled hello while I picked out another Kitty Koller.

Jaylene walked out of the back room and frowned at me. "Did you forget something last time you were here?"

She might as well have tossed a bucket of ice water over me. That was the effect of her cold voice and attitude.

I pointed to the Kitty Koller rack. "No, I just wanted another one of these."

Her attitude didn't change. "That's not the only reason you're here, is it?"

I shrugged. "Well, I did want to ask you some questions."

"I knew it. I knew that's what you were doing. Your mother says you're trying to solve Philip Grenville's murder. To save Abbie from going to jail." She glared at me. "Well, you won't find any suspects here. I told your mother that this morning when she walked in here and started demanding answers to her questions. I've never been so offended in my life."

I wondered what my mother had asked Jaylene. I'd never known her to act so hostile, especially to an old family friend.

"Well, honestly," I said, "I *don't* want my friend to go to jail. So I'm asking questions of everyone I know. I'm not accusing anyone of anything."

Jaylene crossed her arms and stared hard at me. "Well, you'd better not. That's all I have to say."

After my little chat with Gladys, maybe I'd do well to begin with questions about Clark. Not that I could imagine how he would fit into Philip's murder. Still, it would serve to distract Jaylene. "Do you remember those holes in the cat litter bags?"

Her eyes widened. I'd surprised her. "Yes. What about it?"

"Well, I wondered if you knew anything about that

delivery guy. Clark? One of my, um, friends is interested in him. But if he's irresponsible, I want to discourage her." April May *was* a friend. And she *was* interested.

Jaylene relaxed a fraction. "I don't know anything about him except that he's too cocky for someone who works at WWPS. I called them and complained."

"How long has he been coming in here?"

"Only a few weeks. The WWPS company said he was new. Sloppy is what I said."

I pulled some cash from my wallet to pay for the Kitty Koller. "Well, maybe he's not the kind of person she needs to hang out with if you think he hasn't got good character."

She snatched the money from my hand. "Good character is in short supply around here."

I wasn't sure what she meant, but it did remind me of Philip. "Listen, that reminds me that you said Henry had seen Philip in town. I wondered if you knew why he was here."

"Well, why would we know that?" She eyed me with a narrowed glance then slapped some change into my hand. "I'm sure *I* don't know, and Henry wouldn't know, would he? It's not like Philip's a relative of mine or Henry's, is it?"

"Why do you say that?" I asked as I put the money back into my wallet.

She huffed. "He was scum. Just plain scum. But you would know that, wouldn't you? Because of Abbie?"

I couldn't help the look of surprise that I know crossed my face. "Scum?"

She put her hands on her hips. "If I don't hear Philip Grenville's name ever again, I'll be happy. And don't think you can pin this on Henry."

Her vehemence was like a physical blow. "What?"

"Philip's murder. You can't pin that on Henry."

"Why would I pin it on Henry? What does Henry have to do with Philip?"

She glared at me. "Nothing. Absolutely nothing. Isn't that what I said? Now I have things to do, unless you need to buy something else."

My lie-meter alarm, honed from being the mother of five, was clanging like Ma's old dinner bell. Jaylene was covering up something that had to do with Henry and Philip.

I heard some rustling in the back room, then Henry came charging into the store. "Jaylene, I—"

"Trish is just leaving," she said.

Henry finally noticed me. "Trish."

"Henry," I said.

"She's trying to prove that we murdered Philip."

"That's not what I said at all." I couldn't believe how people jumped to conclusions.

Henry's lip curled. "Well, I wouldn't be so ready to defend Abbie. You know she can handle a rifle as easy as a guy can."

"What—"

The door to the shop opened, and Jaylene glanced over my shoulder. Her eyes narrowed.

I turned and saw Clark walking determinedly down the aisle.

"Abbie coulda done it," Henry said, undeterred by the intrusion. "Your daddy taught her, you know."

Clark reached the counter, and Jaylene stood there

with her arms crossed, glaring at him.

"I ain't takin' it back. I called your company and complained. Because you busted open those bags of cat litter."

Clark smiled at her. White teeth. Full wattage. Lit up the room. The guy was good-looking, no doubt about it. "I just came by to apologize," he said. "I'll pay for them."

I watched Jaylene's frown diminish. He was a charmer, all right, if he could accomplish that with her.

"I'll try not to let it happen again." He looked at Henry. "Sir. . ."

Henry nodded.

Then Clark turned to me. His fingertips danced a rhythm against his thighs. His smile faded, and a tiny frown creased the skin between his brows.

"I met you. . . ."

I didn't like the fact that I wasn't memorable. If I were tall and striking like Abbie, he wouldn't have forgotten. "I'm Doris's daughter. Doris's Doughnuts? I met you the other day."

"That's right." He grinned. "I'm headed down there in a minute. Say, you're the one who's gonna take the bookplate to my mother."

I'd be doing that as soon as possible. I wanted to know more about the handsome Clark Matthews. "Yes. I'll do that soon."

"Good. She's excited about it." He looked me up and down. Then he frowned again. "Abbie. Isn't she the one whose husband just—"

"Ex-husband," I snapped. "Yes. He was killed."

"Ah. I'm sorry. Bad thing. You wouldn't think it

would happen around here in Four Oaks." He turned back to Jaylene. "I promise I'll do better in the future. I can't afford to lose my job."

He continued to talk. I edged toward the door. I had a few other things to find out, but I knew one thing for sure. I wasn't going to get any more answers from Jaylene. At least not today.

***

At Doris's Doughnuts, things were hectic. Linda was cleaning a table and chatting with some customers. April May was making sandwiches, and Ma was stomping around the coffee machines, wiping them down hard with a white rag. The scowl on her face was an indication she was in a bad mood. I hoped it wasn't something I'd done.

"Hi, Ma."

She glanced at me. "Well, you came. At least some people do what they say." She slapped the rag on the counter.

I breathed a sigh of relief. That sounded promising. Someone else was the object of her wrath, not me.

"So what's wrong?" I asked. "Oh, and can I have a Mountain Dew, please?"

"What's wrong?" She jammed her fists into her hips. "You ask me what's wrong?"

"Yes," I said. "That's what I asked."

"Well, I'll tell you what. You think people are friends. And then this." She yanked a glass from the stack on the counter and filled it with ice and soda for me.

"Uh-huh." I waited.

When she was done, she slid the glass toward me. "I don't know why I bother."

"Me, either," I murmured to pacify her.

"That's what I get for having friends."

"What happened?" I drew in a mouthful of drink through my straw.

"It's Gail. She called and said she wasn't coming in. Then she said she was taking the rest of the week off."

I almost dropped my glass. "What? She never takes time off except to go to North Carolina once a year."

"Well, people change, now, don't they?" Ma rubbed hard on the counter.

Gail was a legendary stick-in-the-mud. Never altering her routine. That she would suddenly do this meant that things between them were more seriously wrong than I had thought.

"Don't you think you should talk to her?" I asked. "You guys have been friends for years."

"Isn't that what I just said? She shouldn't do this." Ma shook her head. "No. I'm not the one who walked out of here."

While my mother was in this state, I wouldn't be able to convince her to do anything, so maybe a change of topic was in order.

I leaned closer to her so she wouldn't have to talk loudly, although I knew it was a lost cause. "What did you ask Jaylene this morning? She was really upset when I went over there."

"I asked her if she or Henry killed Philip Grenville," Ma said, as loud as ever. "The Adlers have hated Philip forever. I don't know why."

I drew in a deep breath. That was a new low on Ma's lack of subtlety list. And it explained why Jaylene was so hostile. "So if she or Henry had committed murder, you expected her to answer that question honestly?"

Ma blinked. "Well, of course I would. I've known her for years. She goes to church twice a week, and Henry hunts with your father."

I couldn't even think of a reply to that skewed logic, and that was fine because when Ma glanced up over my head, all the tension etching her face melted. She suddenly looked ten years younger. I turned around to see what caused the miracle. I should have guessed. Clark, the studly WWPS man, was walking into the shop.

Seeing him reminded me of Gladys's comments. I could picture Clark as a model, but I didn't want to pursue that further in my head because the pictures weren't edifying. Still, he was from New York. Relatively new in town.

He stopped midway to the counter, and his gaze cut across the room. I followed it. He and Linda were making serious eye contact. She smiled and waved at him. He smiled back then proceeded to the counter and handed some boxes to Ma.

I glanced at April May, who was making a breakfast sandwich behind the counter. I hoped she hadn't noticed the little interchange, but she had. Her arms were frozen. With a roll in one hand and a piece of bacon in the other, she gazed from him to Linda with wide eyes. Then her eyelids dropped. She pursed her lips and set about making the sandwich with deliberate, hard motions. She'd seen exactly what I had seen. Something was going on between Clark and Linda.

I leaned against the counter to watch the soap opera.

Ma, oblivious to everything, just kept chatting with Clark. I heard him compliment her coffee. Linda went back to cleaning tables. April finished the sandwich and, with a stiff back, delivered it to a customer. I felt sorry for her. Clark finished his business, then he smiled at April as she returned to the counter. She just nodded at him and brushed past him and back behind the counter. He frowned. I found myself inwardly cheering for April May.

As he swaggered toward the door to leave, he waved at Linda again, and she held up six fingers. I assumed they were meeting later on.

I watched him leave. Two kids pulled up in front of the shop. He exchanged high fives with them. I turned back to the counter, thinking that outside would be a friendlier place than inside the shop right now.

Ma was swiping her rag across the countertop again.

"You eating?" she asked, back to her grumpy self.

"No," I murmured. "I need to borrow your key to the church."

She glanced sharply at me. "You are going to solve this mystery, aren't you? That's good. It means I don't have to do it myself."

"Yes. I'm looking into it." I wanted to say that I was going to try to solve it if for no other reason than to protect Ma from her own mouth.

"I talked to Abbie, and she told me to put off reception plans, but I'm not going to. I told her that. I told her you'd solve this mystery."

"I'm hoping the police are done at the fellowship hall."

"I'm sure they will be. They assured the pastor they'd be

done as soon as possible. He wants to hold a prayer meeting there this afternoon so people don't feel so strange about being there." She frowned. "They need to do something. The ladies are having a holiday tea on Friday, and a few of the women are going to do some prep work tonight."

I felt sorry for the church members. Their new building was stained, at least figuratively, by a shooting.

"I won't be going," Ma said through narrowed lips.

"Why not?" She'd never missed the tea before.

"Because Gail is in charge."

"Ma, that's child—"

"Wait here," Ma said, cutting me off. "I need to use the bathroom, and then I'll give you my extra fellowship hall key. I can get my other one back from Linda." She strode to the back room.

She knew what I was going to say and didn't want to hear it. Even though it wasn't my fault, I felt bad about the issues between the two women.

Linda had finished talking and wiping tables and was back behind the counter, where she put her rag on the edge of the sink. Then she joined April May, whose mouth was clamped tightly shut. The atmosphere in Doris's Doughnuts was tense today. The only one who didn't seem to notice was Linda.

"You need any help?" Linda asked April with a bright smile on her face—the same one she always used in the hospital emergency room. Was she even aware of how April felt? I remembered what April had said about Linda living in a different dimension.

April gave Linda a sidelong glance then handed her an order form. "Finish this. It's for table three." Then she laid down her knife, wiped her hands, snatched the rag from the sink, and went to bus tables.

Linda stared wide-eyed at April's back, then she began to make the sandwiches. She must have felt my eyes on her because she looked up. "Doris says your friend is a suspect."

"'Person of interest' would be a better term. But then, so am I, and so is my mother. And probably any number of other people."

"I watch those shows on television, and you know what they say. Usually the spouse is the one who's guilty."

April May glanced at me from a table she was cleaning and rolled her eyes. I could pretty safely say she'd joined Gail's "I Don't Like Linda" club.

"Abbie and Philip were divorced a long time ago," I said. "She wasn't his spouse."

Linda leaned toward me. "I saw her signing books at the fall festival. I bought one from her. I've heard some things. I was talking to your mother about it this morning."

"Like what?" I asked.

Her gaze shifted. "I don't want to spread gossip."

Like I believed that. I remembered her big mouth when she worked at the hospital. I'd let her play hard to get. I knew from experience that the best way to get someone to give up a piece of information is to feign disinterest.

"I understand how you feel," I said. "I don't blame you at all for not talking about it." I turned my attention to the bulletin board, where I saw a business card advertising Hayley's purebred Siamese cats.

"People say that Philip was holding something over Abbie," Linda said.

My ruse worked. I barely avoided smiling when I turned back to her. "Like what?"

"I saw them at the festival. They argued. I think he knew some secret about her or something. And because she was making it big with her latest book, he came back to bribe her with something that would ruin her career. Or maybe destroy her new relationship with that detective."

"Like what kind of secret?"

"I'm not sure. Maybe something about why they broke up."

"Oh."

She nodded sagely as though she knew all, then she went back to making sandwiches.

"Does Hayley Whitmore come in here for coffee?" I asked whoever was listening. For some reason, thoughts of her haunted me. I suspected, but didn't want to admit to myself, that my curiosity stemmed from the fact that Hayley was near my age and very close to my mother-in-law.

"Yeah," April said. "Like twice a week. She says we make her laugh."

Along with me, my mother and her cohorts were amusing to Hayley. I wondered if she and Angelica made fun of all of us while they sipped iced tea at the country club.

Ma returned with a key dangling between her fingers. "Here you go. The key to the church hall. I'll need it back, but I'm glad you're doing this. Visiting the murder scene. What are you looking for?"

"I don't know." I glanced around the full shop. Coming here had been stupid. At this point, anyone could have murdered Philip. I didn't need my plans advertised. Of course, Ma would advertise them anyway. I needed to be careful what I told her.

"Well now, that's not smart. You need a plan." Ma frowned. "You need to look for evidence. Like in the corners of things. Somebody was out there before we got there. Somebody killed Philip, and it wasn't Abbie, even though, heaven knows, she had every reason to. Especially if he was threatening her."

"Ma, you don't know that. And I'm sure the police have gathered all the evidence there is to gather."

"Police." She made a rude sound. "Well, why else was Philip there if he wasn't threatening her? What in the world was he doing back in Four Oaks?"

That was the question I intended to answer. And I hoped I could do it before my mother inadvertently convinced the whole town that Abbie had offed Philip.

8

My next stop was to see Eric. When I walked through the doors at the sheriff's office, I felt a tremor of apprehension as I recalled my interview the night before with Detective Reid. The fact that I was here again on my own accord was a testimony to my love for my best friend.

The girl behind a wall of bulletproof glass at the front desk called Eric and then told me to have a seat. Shortly after that, a deputy came to escort me and buzzed me through a locked door. When we reached Eric's office, he was sitting at his desk. Pain so twisted his face, I felt like a voyeur looking at him.

"Sir?" the deputy said.

Eric glanced up and grimaced with what was probably supposed to be a smile. "Trish. Please come in."

"Hey," I said as I dropped into a chair in front of his desk. The deputy shut the door.

I noticed some new pictures displayed on his credenza. His and Abbie's engagement pictures. He, Abbie, and his daughter, Sherry, were all grinning broadly. My heart ached.

"Have you talked to Sherry?" I asked.

He drew a deep breath. "I'd planned to call her as soon as I talked to you. I don't want her to hear about this before I tell her. This is the end of her first college term. I hate that it might affect her exams."

"It's going to be hard on her," I said. "She'll be frantic with worry."

"I know," he said softly. "She's so excited I'm marrying Abbie."

I leaned forward and put my elbows on his desk. "You wanted to talk to me?"

He sighed. "Yes."

"Before we start, can you tell me if Philip's death is a murder?" I asked.

"Suspicious," he said.

"But that's always the way it is, right?" I asked. "With an unexpected violent death like this?"

"Yes." He brushed his fingers through his hair.

"Detective Reid is not on my top-ten list of people to invite to Christmas dinner."

One side of his mouth quirked. "A number of people feel that way."

"So Corporal Fletcher said the state police are involved to avoid conflict of interest. I'm not sure that makes sense to me, but I understand what it means."

He sighed. "It's just to keep things from being muddled. If we investigate, Abbie might be given some sort of preferential treatment, and important evidence could be overlooked."

"Why is preferential treatment a big deal? Especially when we both know she didn't do it?"

"A suspect could get off in court if a lawyer can prove we didn't handle an investigation correctly."

"Are all the state police people as friendly as Detective Reid? Do you know any of them?"

"I know some of them," he said. "And friendly? Define friendly."

"That's a good point," I said. "They are, after all, cops."

He narrowed his eyes. "What does that mean?"

"Surface friendly, but underneath you're suspicious of everyone. Always looking for bad guys. You're out to nail our hides to the wall."

That made him smile. "Yes and no. We're trained to observe. We can't afford blanket trust in people. And in suspicious circumstances, we have to look at everyone involved as a person of interest. Our jobs make us that way. If you were lied to as much as we are, you'd be the same." He paused. "Besides, we're not all just surface friendly. Look at me. Look at Fletcher."

I rolled my eyes. "Please, Eric. I remember when I first met you."

"Well, at first, you were a person of interest in a murder case. You wouldn't expect me to be friendly." He eyed me with a slight smile. "And you—"

"Didn't tell you the whole truth. I know." My face grew warm. "But I didn't lie, either. I just avoided the truth."

"See?"

"Yeah, well, whatever." I didn't like to remember that I had tried to deceive Eric during Jim Bob's murder investigation. "Anyway, I don't like the way this is going at all." I tap-danced my fingers on the chair arms. "The state police people aren't going to care about Abbie."

He smiled grimly. "That's the whole point of having them investigate."

"Will they question all of us again?"

"No doubt," he said.

"So what's the procedure for something like this?" I asked. "How long do they investigate at the scene?"

He eyed me. "In this case, I assume they were back

there first thing this morning, but I. . . They aren't talking to me about it. It's a tough scene, though. The shooter was way off in the woods. They had to comb the whole area."

"Do you think they're done now?"

He glanced at his watch. "I imagine. They were getting a lot of pressure from the church people because there's some big event coming up, and they need the building."

"Yeah. It's a ladies' holiday tea."

He nodded. "That's right." Then he suddenly squinted at me. "Why do you want to know?"

I shrugged. "Just curious. So what did you want to talk about?"

"Abbie," he said.

"I sort of figured." I settled back in the chair and crossed my legs. "What do you want to discuss about her?"

He met my gaze with tired eyes. "She's withdrawn. She's talking about canceling the wedding. I don't know what to do because she won't talk to me. Is she talking to you?"

"In dibs and dabs, but probably a little more than she's talking to you."

"That wouldn't be hard," he said dryly.

"Her reaction doesn't surprise me," I said. "She's always been that way. When she's in pain, she withdraws."

"It's killing me. I need her to talk to me." I saw a flash of anger in his eyes. "Does she think she's the only one this is impacting?"

I shook my head. "No. Not at all. And that's why she's withdrawn. She's worried she's going to affect your career. And I think underneath, she's worried that you're mad."

"Well, truthfully, I am." He stood and paced the length of his desk. "Why couldn't she have told me that

Philip had contacted her? I look like an idiot." He stopped and inhaled, then met my gaze. "I'm not allowed to have any part in this investigation. I don't know much of what's going on, and she won't even confide in me. Do you know how frustrating that is?"

"Yes, I can imagine." I thought of all the times he hadn't answered my questions. I could be childish and point that out, but instead, I felt compassion for him.

Eric dropped into his chair, grabbed a pen, and started tapping it on the desktop. A vein in his temple pulsed. He was much more worried than he was letting on.

"So you don't know why Philip was in town, then?" I asked.

His gaze slid over me, then to his desk, then back to me. "I don't know why he was in town, but. . .I did know he was here."

I grasped the arms of my chair. "You did? And you didn't tell Abbie? Eric, what's the difference between you not telling her and her not telling you?"

"Plenty," he said. "For one thing, he wasn't hounding me."

I had to give him that. "Do you know what he was doing?"

"Well, I knew he had been visiting his mother. He did that periodically. And I always kept track of him because I *didn't* want him bugging Abbie. We usually talked about our investigations. Like I told him I'd recently been assigned to work with Narcotics on a special case." Eric stopped and drew in a deep breath. "Trish, you have to understand that I was concerned about him. I wanted to protect Abbie, but I was still concerned about Philip. That's why I kept in contact with him. I wanted more than anything for him to get his life straightened out."

"I understand," I said softly.

"The strange thing is, he called me and left a message the day he was shot. Just said he wanted to talk to me— had something to tell me." Eric tapped his pen harder. "I was in a class, but I wish I'd answered. Maybe he wouldn't have died."

"When did he call you?" I asked.

"Based on everything I know now, about an hour before he was shot."

I made a mental note about that because the timing was curious. "I know he moved to New York City. Has he been there all this time?"

Eric nodded. "Yes. He was working for the NYPD. He did pretty well. Moved up the ladder. Worked as a detective and in Narcotics. Made lieutenant. Never married again, just had a string of girlfriends."

Eric sighed. "You know he was a good friend when we were in the academy together, right?"

I nodded.

"Then he was a fellow officer. There's something about that. A camaraderie that I can't explain." Eric's eyes boring into mine seemed to beg me to understand, then he looked away. "When he was first married to Abbie, things were fine. But after a while, I began to realize things weren't right. Eventually I saw what he was doing with other women." He rubbed the skin between his eyebrows. "She came to me and tried to talk to me about some things. I blew her off. He was my friend. A fellow cop. A brother of sorts. That hurt her bad."

"I know," I said. "I'm just glad she got over it and is

giving you a chance now. Neither one of you is the same person you were back then."

"Yes." For a moment, his face brightened, and then the light died.

I decided a change of subject would be good. "Philip's timing in being here is interesting, don't you think?"

Eric's eyes focused on me again. "Well, I wouldn't say 'interesting' is the best choice of words, given how things have turned out. More like disturbing."

"There has to be a reason he was here," I said. "I just wish Abbie had me or Daddy with her when Philip first approached her. We could have helped."

"I wish she had, too. Things might have been different." He glanced at the desk then up at me. "Do you know something I don't know about Abbie? A secret reason she could have had to murder Philip? Or have him murdered?"

"What?" I shot forward in my chair. "Do you mean you think she did it? I can't believe it. What are you—"

"No!" He stretched out his right hand as if he were directing traffic and telling me to stop. "Please, Trish. I know her better than that. But she is very deep. I know there are layers in her that I haven't begun to see. I just don't want something coming to light that will hurt her." He rubbed his eyes. "I don't want someone else discovering something."

"Like the bulldog, you mean?" I took a deep breath. "You want me to look into things?"

He met my gaze with wide eyes. "You're kidding, right?"

A brief surge of irritation washed over me. "Do I look like I'm kidding? This is a serious conversation, is it not?"

"Yes, it is a serious conversation, and no, you don't look like you're kidding. I was being facetious. I know perfectly well how you are. In fact, you're probably already looking into things. That's why you wanted to know about the crime scene."

I felt warmth on my cheeks.

"I'm right, aren't I?" he asked. "And you have one of those notebooks in your purse, don't you?"

Body language plays a big part in police interrogation and interviewing. Mine gave me up.

"You do," he said. "Admit it."

"Yes, I do."

"Trish, you need to stay out of this." He shifted in his chair and it creaked. "For a number of reasons."

I shook my head. "My best friend is a suspect. I can't let this go."

"I'm asking you to. She'll be fine." Even as he said it, I could tell he wasn't sure he believed it himself.

I felt angry all over again when I thought of Abbie huddled on her couch, crying. "You weren't there after she was interviewed. You didn't see the shape she was in." I described how I found her the night before.

Eric blinked. "She never told me that."

"Well, of course she didn't. She doesn't want to compromise you." I placed my hands on his desk. "I know I can do this."

He leaned back in his chair. "I know you can, too, but there's so much at stake. Your getting involved could make a messy situation messier—not to mention being dangerous for you."

I wasn't going to press the point. I already knew what

I was going to do. And I wondered before all this ended if Eric might welcome my help.

His phone rang.

"Excuse me," he said. After a few uh-huhs and glances at me, he put the phone down. "Detective Reid would like to see you. She's here in the building, and she's sending someone to get you."

"How did she know I was here?"

"The walls have eyes." A grim smile passed over his face. "I think I'm going to need to watch my step."

⚊⚊

As I waited for Detective Reid in the bland interview room, I remembered the first time I had been here, interviewed by Eric. At the time, I'd thought that was a bad situation. Things had certainly gone from bad to worse. After being kept waiting what I presumed was a suitable amount of time to keep me off balance, Detective Reid walked in.

"Good morning, Mrs. Cunningham."

"Hello." I put my elbows on the table and stared at her.

She dropped onto a chair across from me. "I'd just like to go over your statement again."

I nodded.

She pulled out a piece of paper and read each answer I'd given her. Each time she looked up at me, I nodded.

"Well, that's about it," she said as she stood.

I waited. I had a feeling I was about to find out her real purpose for asking me here.

As she gathered her papers in her arms, she glanced at her telephone then back at me. "Why were you here today?"

I had to tread carefully, and I wasn't sure what to say. I didn't want to put Eric on the spot, although I had a feeling he already was.

"I came to see Eric Scott."

"About?"

"He's about to marry my best friend. He was concerned about her well-being because he hasn't seen her since Philip died."

"He hasn't seen her?" The surprise was evident on Detective Reid's face, but she got control of herself quickly.

"No."

"Mmm." She headed toward the door.

I braced myself, thinking about Lieutenant Columbo on television. He used to do the same thing. Make the suspect feel like they were home free, then turn around and fire questions. I wasn't disappointed. She whirled around to face me again.

"Were you aware that Abbie Grenville met Philip Grenville at the Gas 'n' Go the day he was murdered?"

"Yes," I said.

"You didn't tell me this yesterday," she said, her flat, cold eyes nailing me to the chair.

"I didn't know yesterday," I said.

She nodded very slowly. "I see. And where did you find this out?"

"From Abbie," I said.

"And when did you speak to her?"

"Last night," I said.

"I see." Detective Reid put her hand on the doorknob. "Is there anything else you know that you believe would be pertinent to the case?"

I shrugged. "I have no idea what I know that you think might be pertinent."

The detective smiled grimly. "You have quite the reputation."

I stood, picked up my purse, and slung it over my shoulder. "I've lived in Four Oaks all my life. I'm sure you're going to hear all sorts of things about me."

She stared down at me. "Don't get in my way, Mrs. Cunningham. This is not a game of Sherlock Holmes. *I* don't appreciate civilians getting involved in my investigations."

"Frankly, Detective Reid, I don't know any law enforcement officer who does like civilians involved in their investigations."

She stared at me with narrowed eyes.

Detective Reid was a formidable foe. She smiled slowly, looking like a shark, then motioned for me to go ahead of her so she could escort me from the building.

I returned her smile as I passed her and saw a flicker in her eye. I had a feeling this wasn't the last of my little chats with the detective.

9

I stopped to eat lunch at Bo's Burger Barn, but I didn't have much of an appetite. When I ended up pushing my onion rings around the half-eaten cheeseburger on my plate, I realized it was pointless. I wasn't going to finish. I shoved the whole thing aside and pulled the steno pad out of my purse. I needed to write notes about what I had learned that morning.

I looked at what I'd already written about Philip. To that, I added:

Philip called Eric an hour before he was shot.

Then I flipped a few pages ahead, titled the page "Suspects," and began to write.

Jaylene and Henry Adler. They hated Philip. Why? And why is Jaylene so defensive that Henry had nothing to do with Philip's murder?
Clark Matthews? New in town. Worked in New York City as a "model." Could have had a run-in with Philip there.

He just didn't seem like a viable suspect to me, but I had so little to go on, I needed to follow every lead I had.

I tried to take a sip of my Mountain Dew and sucked up nothing through the straw but water from the melted ice. I'd been here a long time. I was avoiding my next stop.

It was the one I was dreading. Back to the murder scene.

My cell phone rang as I finished paying for my lunch. I looked at the screen. It was Eric's daughter, Sherry.

"Hi, hon," I said as I walked out into the cold air. I tugged my coat tight around me.

"Mrs. C.!" She was yelling so loud, I had to pull the phone away from my ear. "You'vegottosolvethismysteryso DadcanmarryAbbie!"

Sherry was frantic. I understood. That was how I felt on the inside. "I guess you talked to your father?"

"Yes! And I need to come home, but he won't let me."

I jammed the phone between my head and my shoulder and dug through the mess in my purse for my keys. I needed to clean it out. "There's not much you could do here," I said. "It doesn't make sense for you to miss school. And you need to calm down. Getting hysterical isn't going to help."

I heard her take a deep breath. "I'm sorry."

"It's fine. I understand totally. This has been a nightmare."

"So are you going to solve this?"

"I'm going to try." I unlocked my SUV and climbed in. The sun had been shining through the windows, and I was grateful for the relative warmth of the interior.

"I'm going to call you when I can," she said. "And Tommy might have some ideas, too. I talked to him."

"That's fine. I can use all the input I can get."

Unlike Detective Reid, I welcomed help from any source. And a college student at a distance might have a different perspective.

Sherry interrogated me for the next twenty minutes

while I drove to the fellowship hall. I told her everything I knew. Then we said our good-byes.

Before I reached the fellowship hall, I turned onto the road Abbie had told me about. The one that passed around the church property and would have allowed someone access through the woods to the back of the property where Philip had been shot. I drove slowly and noticed a dirt road leading back into the trees. If I had my bearings right, this headed toward the hall.

I pulled my SUV into the entrance, trying to avoid tree limbs that threatened to scrape the paint off the side of my vehicle. The road narrowed, and the woods closed in around me. I stopped. Perhaps this was only a parking place for hunters or kids.

If nothing else, this isolated spot would have made a great hiding place for a vehicle while the murderer shot Philip. I wished I could investigate more, but I felt uneasy. I backed up, pulled onto the road, and headed for the fellowship hall.

The yellow police tape had been removed from the church property. Things looked normal. I let myself into the building. I wasn't really expecting to find anything. I was sure the police had been thorough. I just wanted to get a sense of things. Maybe some flash of insight.

I looked all over the kitchen. In corners and cupboards. But I found nothing. Then I leaned against the kitchen island and tried to imagine what had happened. What had Philip done after Abbie left for McDonald's? Why had he gone to the backyard of the church?

I mentally shook myself. I was only postponing the inevitable. Going outside. Where a single shot from a rifle had ended Philip's life.

As I walked down the steps, I averted my gaze from where Philip had bled to death. Instead, I glanced up into the woods. Who had been up there? I could almost imagine eyes gazing at me.

I heard the distant sound of a car engine, and it brought me back to reality. After a stabilizing breath, I approached the spot where Philip's body had been. I hated the thought that he had died so unexpectedly. As he died, had he known it was the end? Had he known the Lord?

I glanced up at the woods. A breeze whispered through the bare trees, and I shivered in my coat. This spot was so isolated. A great place to commit a murder. I wondered what the police looked at. There was something called a line of sight, I thought, but I knew very little about crime scene investigation.

The sound of the car engine came closer; then I heard a vehicle pull in front of the building. The engine stopped. Then a car door opened and slammed shut.

I felt a brief surge of panic, thinking maybe I should hide. But that was silly. My SUV was parked right out front. Besides, the scene had been cleared. I could conceivably be here for church business.

Squaring my shoulders, I jogged up the back stairs, mentally fortifying my excuses for being here. I yanked the door open and came face-to-face with Corporal Fletcher.

"Mrs. C.," he said as he moved aside and made a motion for me to enter the room.

I'd never seen him angry, but there was no doubt that at this moment, he was furious. At me. Under his bushy brows, his eyes were emitting sparks. All the reasons for my presence here fled my brain.

He shut the back door with more force than necessary then settled his full gaze on me. "Didn't I tell you to stay away from all of this?"

I felt as if the fire from his eyes was burning my retinas as we stared at each other. "Yes, you did, but I needed to, um, do something for, uh, my mother. . . ." My voice trailed away.

The slight shaking of his head told me he saw right through my half-truth. "I was not joking when I told you to stay away."

I have the unfortunate inability to stay intimidated for long, and the corporal's anger triggered my self-defense mechanism. "I'm not a child, Corporal Fletcher. And I'm not here just playing around."

He took a deep breath. "I know why you're here. Eric told me you'd been to his office. And you offered to investigate."

"He told you that?"

"Yes. And he also told me that he tried to dissuade you. And yet here you are."

"How did you know I was coming *here*?"

"Because you asked him if the state police were through with the scene. And I also happened to see you from the woods."

"You mean. . ."

"Yeah. I was up in the woods looking things over." The sparks in his eyes had turned to flaming embers. "You got any idea how easy it would have been to pick you off? If I had been someone with, let's say, bad intentions? Like maybe the same person who shot a hole in Philip

Grenville?" His voice had risen to a loud growl.

I swallowed then felt unexpected tears prickle my eyelids, so I looked down at my feet. To have kindhearted Corporal Fletcher so angry with me hurt.

"Mrs. C., can't you understand what I'm saying? I got too much to worry about right now without you in the mix. I don't have time for this." He turned away from me and began pacing.

I let him pace for a minute or so, hoping it would calm him down. Then I glanced up at him. He stopped walking and met my gaze. I felt a tear run down my cheek.

"Aw, man." His bunched facial muscles relaxed, and the flame in his eyes died. "I made you cry." He swore under his breath. "I'm sorry."

I shook my head and sniffled. "It isn't just you. I'm so worried. Abbie is my closest friend. In some ways, she's closer to me than Max. She finally has a chance to be happy. . . ." I gripped the kitchen island tightly with my hands. "That wedding has got to happen."

"That's the way I feel about Eric." Corporal Fletcher eyed me for a long time, and I could tell he was deciding whether he wanted to say anything else to me.

I waited.

"I'm here doing what you're doing," he said finally. "I'm here on my own time, and I'm telling you 'cause I don't want Eric to know. I don't want *anyone* to know, including Abbie. I could get in trouble. You gotta promise me, Mrs. C."

"You're not going to tell Eric?"

The corporal shook his head. "No way. He's my commanding officer. He can't know. He'd have to order me to stop. I wouldn't want to break my word to him. And I wouldn't want him to get in trouble for what I'm doing."

"Okay. You've got my word." The corporal's confession surprised me, yet at the same time it didn't. "So you're really doing the same thing I am? Trying to help Abbie and Eric?"

"Yes. At the risk of being charged with misconduct and insubordination if someone finds out."

"But you were here the night they were collecting evidence. Why did you come back today? What more could you find out? Do you think they did a sloppy job investigating?"

He shook his head. "I don't think they missed anything, but I wanted to revisit the scene. Just to think about what happened." He motioned toward the back door. "I'm going to look out there."

"You mind if I come?"

"Nope. Glad for the company."

I felt much safer with the corporal along. I stayed quiet so as not to disturb him. He stood looking up into the woods.

"Great place for a shooting," he finally said. "Easy access. Easy escape."

"But why was Philip out here?" I asked. "Why was his car parked down the road? Abbie said when she left that he was out front."

He glanced at me. "That's one of my questions. Doesn't make much sense, does it? Unless someone made him come out here. Or walked out here with him." Corporal Fletcher took a deep breath. "That's the thing. Who knew he was here? This was at least slightly premeditated. Even if someone by chance had a gun in the trunk of their car, they still had to know Philip was out here alone and then hide their car and shoot him. You see why it looks bad for Abbie? And why Eric is concerned even though he won't admit it?"

My stomach rolled into a knot. "Yep, I see. And I don't even know who the suspects are. The other times I've been involved with a murder, they were obvious. This time the only obvious suspect is Abbie, and I know she's not guilty."

"You know that. I know that. Eric knows that, but she's lookin' real good as a suspect, Mrs. C. If I was the lead on this case, I'd be lookin' pretty close at her. There's stuff that points at her, and—"

My mouth went dry. "Like what?"

He shifted from one foot to the other. "Not sure I can tell you that. Don't want to be accused of compromising the investigation."

I wanted to stomp my feet and scream that the investigation was already compromised if they were looking at Abbie.

Corporal Fletcher's attention had left me, and he was looking at the ground where Philip's body had been. I refused to look down.

"Mm-hmm," he said. Then he knelt.

The thought of kneeling anywhere near where the blood had been made me feel like the onion rings, cheeseburger, and Mountain Dew were congealing in my stomach. I turned my face toward the woods and tried to clear my mind.

"This is interesting," Corporal Fletcher said. I glanced at his head out of the corner of my eye. He stood and wiped his knees with one hand and held out something for me to see with the other. "They found some of this the other night. I wanna know what you think."

That got my attention. "That looks like a tiny piece of. . .gravel. . .wait." I bent over his hand. "That's cat litter. I know because I just bought some for Sammie's new kitten."

He grinned. "A clue for you, Mrs. C."

"Cat litter." I thought about the Adlers.

The corporal's eyes narrowed. "You got a thought about this, don't you?" He dropped the piece of litter and stared at me.

I shrugged. "I'm not sure."

"Okay, we'll come back to that in a minute. Right now I want you to think back about the body."

My stomach lurched. "I don't want to. I feel like throwing up."

Corporal Fletcher nodded. "I understand. Just try to think of it as a body, not a person."

My mind didn't seem to want to make that differentiation, but I took a deep breath and ordered my stomach to behave. "Okay."

"Did you see his face?"

"How am I supposed to think of it as just a body when you want me to think about his face?" I snapped.

Corporal Fletcher patted my arm again. "I'm sorry. I wouldn't ask if it wasn't important. So did you see his face?"

I swallowed hard. "Yes. For a few seconds."

"Anything you noticed? Different from a normal face?"

I thought about it. Philip's eyes had been closed. And there had been some discoloration around his eye. I looked up at Corporal Fletcher. "Like. . .bruises? Maybe a black eye?"

He nodded. "Good so far."

"Oh, I see. This is a guessing game. It's a clue. Evidence. But you're not going to tell me. So you can't be accused of compromising anything."

"You got it."

I bit my lip and thought about it. Then I realized what he was getting at. "Someone hit Philip. And it wasn't at the time of his murder. It was before."

Corporal Fletcher smiled. "Smart cookie."

I felt proud, like I'd passed a test. "So someone was possibly angry enough at him to hit him. And that same person could have been angry enough to kill him."

"Bingo. And you figured it out yourself. I didn't tell you."

Black eye. Fight. Anger. Once again, I thought of the Adlers.

As if he could read my face and knew I had some suspicions, Corporal Fletcher motioned to the stairs. "Let's go inside and talk."

I glanced around, suddenly feeling uncomfortable. "You know, it would be just as easy for someone to shoot both of us out here."

He smiled. "I've been listening for cars. Haven't heard a thing."

Back inside the church hall, we stood in the kitchen. I was on one side of the island, and he was on the other.

"You're not going to stop looking into this, are you?" he asked.

Feeling a little bit like Charlie when he was rebelling, I crossed my arms. "No, I'm not going to stop looking into this."

"You got one of those notebooks in your purse, don't you?"

"Yes." I glared at him. "Yes, I do." It was annoying that he and Eric knew me so well.

He held up his hand, placating me. "It's okay." His gaze was searching. "I trust you, Mrs. C. You're good people. And you got good instincts, too. Seeing as how I can't stop you from doing this, how about a partnership?"

"Partnership? Just a few minutes ago you were lecturing me about being involved. Now you want to partner with me?"

"Well, I can change my mind." He paced the kitchen again. "I got my reasons. Among them, it'll be easier to keep tabs on you. Plus, you can find out things that I can't." He stopped pacing and stared at me. "And that way, you have to tell me what *you* know."

"And in turn, that means you'll have to tell me what you know?"

At his pause, I knew this wasn't going to be an equal deal. That figured. "Why should I partner with you when you aren't going to share with me?"

"I'll be straight with you, Mrs. C. It's bad enough I'm doing this on my own time. But I got certain rules I won't cross. One of them is sharing official evidence in an investigation. Not that I'm going to know all the evidence. But still, even if I told you what I know, that could jeopardize the case."

"Well, I won't—"

"Okay, I'll put it this way. If it ever came out that I

was telling you things only the cops know, a murderer could go free, and I could lose my job and my pension. But if it's something you could easily know, I'll tell you. Or we'll play another guessing game."

I had to understand that. "Can I at least tell Max?"

Corporal Fletcher blinked.

"He's worried sick about my doing this. It would relieve his mind, and he won't tell a soul."

Corporal Fletcher studied me then finally nodded. "I'll trust you two. Just remember. This could really hurt my career."

That's when I realized how much Eric meant to Corporal Fletcher. That he would go to this length to help him said a lot about their friendship. I could relate to that kind of loyalty. Abbie and Eric had to succeed with two good friends who would risk everything for them.

"All right. I agree. We'll work together." I suddenly felt like Watson to his Sherlock Holmes.

"Okay, so spill. What's in that notebook of yours?"

I pulled out my notebook and read my few clues to him. Then I told him about the Adlers and the kitty litter.

"I can look into that," he said. "See if there's something someone knows. Be careful, Mrs. C. Sounds like they're angry."

"They're definitely that," I said. "And I'm sorry. I don't know a lot yet."

"But it's a beginning."

"So I guess I'll call you when I learn anything," I said.

"Yes. I'll give you my cell phone number." He pulled out a business card and a pen and jotted his number on the back. Then he handed it to me.

He grinned at me. "This is very unusual for me. To ask for help from someone like you."

"Someone like me?"

"A civilian who isn't an informant. It's against all proper procedure."

I smiled back. "Well, you'll find me to be a good partner." I paused. "Can you tell me if Abbie is the only person of interest?"

He shrugged. "She's looking the best. There might be others, but I don't know for sure. Since this went to the state, I'm not privy to much."

A few minutes later, I watched him climb into his car. As I opened the door to my SUV, I looked down at the gravel. A gold-colored button lay flattened on the ground. I wondered if it was Abbie's. I picked it up. Too bad. But a flattened button was the least of her worries.

10

Before I pulled out of the parking lot, I glanced at my watch. I had a little more time before I had to pick up Chris. I wanted to find out how Abbie was doing. I called her and she picked up right away, which surprised me.

"Hi," I said. "Are you okay?"

"Better than last night in some ways, but I need to talk to you."

"I'm on my way to your house right now."

Twenty minutes later, I was in her living room. She had applied makeup and was dressed in a nice pair of jeans and a tailored shirt, all of which was a good sign because it meant she was trying to regain some control of her life. However, the circles under her bloodshot eyes and the drawn expression on her face told the real story.

After I hugged her, I looked around. She had made an effort to straighten up. I was glad for that because it meant she had some fight in her.

"Have you eaten anything?" I asked.

"I forced myself to eat lunch—some of what your mother sent over," she said.

"Good," I said. "You want me to make some coffee or tea?"

She shook her head.

"Okay." I dropped into a chair and put my purse at my feet. "I've been to see Eric."

"I know. He called and told me." She swallowed and blinked. "He doesn't say so, but I can hear in his voice that he's angry with me for not telling him about Philip."

"Do you blame him? I was a little irritated myself. You do have a habit of keeping things to yourself."

"You're right." She took a deep breath. "And I'm trying. That's why I asked you to come. Because I need to come clean and tell you everything."

My heart plummeted. "What do you mean, *everything*? Abbie, what else could there be?" I realized immediately how harsh I'd sounded. "I'm sorry. I didn't mean that."

"Yes, you did." She stuck her chin in the air. "And I suppose you've told me every little detail about your life? There's *nothing* I don't know?"

Some color had returned to her face. Perhaps the two of us semiquarreling wasn't a bad thing.

"Okay," I said. "You have a point. Except that I'm not a suspect in a murder."

"And that's why I'm telling you this. Because I am— now. I wasn't before."

That made sense in an odd way. "Have you told Eric what you're about to tell me?"

"I sent him an e-mail. I haven't heard back." She was pumping her leg up and down, a nervous habit she'd had since she was a kid. She had tried to conquer it as an adult, but the bouncing returned when she was stressed out.

"Philip wrote me a letter two weeks ago. I returned it to him unopened. With a letter of my own telling him to leave me alone. I know it sounded. . .almost threatening."

"And the police found it?"

"Yes. He had it with him at his mother's house."

"So you didn't look at his letter at all?"

"No. I just didn't want to be reminded of the past." She picked up a pillow and put it in her lap. "You remember back then, right?"

"Yeah, I do," I said.

"I thought we'd be happy forever," Abbie murmured. "I thought he loved me. But then I started hearing all the rumors of other women."

I nodded but didn't speak. I couldn't because I still carried some anger in my heart against the man—now dead—who had devastated my best friend.

"Um, the last couple of times I confronted him, he hit me." She wouldn't meet my gaze.

"Hit you?" I felt like *I'd* been punched. "He hit you? And you never told me?"

She blushed but looked defensive, too. "I was so humiliated at the time, dealing with his infidelities. Like everyone was staring at me. And it only happened a couple of times."

"But I'm your best friend. Why couldn't you tell me? Eric asked me today if there were things in your past that you were keeping secret. I assured him there weren't, but you're like a book of secrets."

"I was so young at the time. He was a cop. He wore a badge and carried a gun. When he spoke, people listened. He held that over my head. You know. . .while we were married, he used to tell me that he could. . .make me disappear? I was terrified."

I was gritting my teeth and trying not to hate a dead man. "So what happened? I know he supposedly just walked out of your life. Is that really how it went?"

"Yes, pretty much. Well, I took pictures of the last

batch of bruises he left on me. I made copies and put them in a safe-deposit box, but I didn't need them." She frowned. "Something else happened. I'm not sure what, but he came home in an unusual mood one night. Unfocused. Maybe a little scared. He methodically started packing a suitcase. Said he was leaving me and leaving town."

"That was good, right?"

"Well, yes, but weird, too. I didn't understand. But that's when I did the first thing I can say makes me proud. I went immediately to a lawyer and filed for divorce. He assured me that with the proof I had, I was fine. Then I went home, packed up the rest of Philip's things, put them in the garage, and changed the locks on the house. I had him served with the papers. I also sent him a letter."

"A letter?"

"Yes. Unfortunately, that letter was even more hostile than the one I just sent him two weeks ago. I basically threatened him with retaliation if he tried to talk to me again."

"Violence?"

"No." She inhaled. "But I didn't say exactly what. I don't remember what I said, but it was something along the lines of 'If you bother me again, I will make sure it's the last time.' I meant, of course, that I would drag him into court.

"But, Trish, he kept the letter, along with the divorce papers. The investigators found it, too, along with the one I sent him two weeks ago. Between the two of those letters, I pretty much spelled out exactly what he had done to me back then. So the police know everything."

"Oh boy." I didn't know what else to say, but I

understood why Detective Reid was looking so closely at Abbie. Suspicion of revenge.

"Maybe you don't understand," Abbie said softly. "It's been nine years. When I suddenly got a letter out of the blue and then Philip showed up and started following me, I panicked. I realized I was still afraid of him."

"I can understand that," I said.

"You know what's really bad?" Abbie bit down on her lower lip.

"Um, everything?"

That earned me an eye roll from her, despite the seriousness of the topic. "My emotions. They're so mixed. That's making the interviews and everything harder, because I walk in there feeling bad and walk out even worse off."

"The system is designed to break you down," I said.

"Yes, I know that, but this is much deeper." Her fingers spasmodically clutched at the pillow in her lap. "I feel like such a bad person to even say this, but there was a part of me that was relieved Philip was dead. That meant there was no potential for him to contact me again. I could finally really and truly move on." She glanced at me. "That's horrible, isn't it?"

"No," I said. "Normal, I think. Remember how I felt a bit of relief when Jim Bob died?"

Some of the tension on her face left. "I'd forgotten that. But. . .here's where it gets all mixed up." She pulled the pillow to her chest as if to protect herself. "After that initial feeling of relief, I was hit with horrible sorrow. Like I'd lost the marriage all over again. And then I wondered if there was more I could have done to make it work. Was it my fault? And was I responsible for his not following the Lord?" She hiccuped and swallowed. "The guilt has been unbelievable. And it's made me wonder if everything that's happening now is some kind of judgment from God. That I don't deserve. . .Eric. . .or happiness. . ." She dropped her head into the pillow and cried silently, shoulders shaking.

That I couldn't hear her cries made them all the worse. I began to cry, too, and scooted over to the sofa to hold her.

"I'm sorry," I murmured as I rubbed her back. "I'm so, so sorry."

After several minutes, I felt her sobs die. She inhaled, and I knew she was done.

I sat back and handed her another tissue. "You're probably going to have to wash that pillow."

She smiled weakly. "It is a mess, isn't it?" She laid it back on her lap. "I'm sorry for being such a wreck."

"Don't you ever apologize to me for anything like that." I clenched my fists, wanting to pound on something. "Abbie, this is *not* God's judgment. You don't *really* believe that, do you?"

"In the darkest night, I do." She paused and frowned. "In the light of day? Maybe I don't then. I'm just so tired and worn out from all the questions. I feel like I've been. . .battered."

Enough was enough. I grabbed my purse, yanked my notebook and pen from its depths, and settled back on the couch.

Abbie's face brightened. "You really are going to try to solve this? Eric said you might. And he also said he told you not to."

"Has that ever stopped me before?" I asked.

"No. And I have to say at this point, I'm relieved."

I wished I could tell her that Corporal Fletcher was working with me, because that would double her sense of security, but I couldn't.

"Do you think I would let you do this alone?" I held the pen over the steno pad. "I can't be there in the interview room with you to protect you from the bulldog, but I can try to solve this mystery so she'll leave you alone." I grinned. "I could take her, you know."

Abbie did break a smile for that. "Oh, I'm sure you could."

The atmosphere momentarily lightened. I sat back. "Let's get busy. Is there anything else you think would help me?"

"I've been thinking a lot about the fall festival, where I first saw Philip," Abbie said. "He was acting odd there. I didn't realize it at the time because I was so traumatized to see him and distracted with signing my books. But I realized he left very abruptly after he mumbled something about getting back to me."

I tapped my pen on my notebook. "This could have something to do with the past." I told Abbie about the Adlers.

She nodded. "They did hate him. I was never sure why."

I had a sudden, brilliant idea. "Do you think his mother would talk to me? June?"

Abbie's face lit up. "Yes, I think she would."

"Will you call her and ask her and then let me know? Would you feel awkward doing that?"

"No. We do talk now and then."

"Do you want to go with me to see her?"

Abbie shook her head violently. "No. She and I have already agreed that to see each other right now would be too emotional."

I glanced at my watch. "I need to get Charlie at the YMCA. He's there with Mike. I also need to pick up Chris from the sitter. And Sammie will be home shortly. Oh." I reached into my purse, pulled out the button, and held it out to her. "I found one of your buttons in the parking lot of the church hall. It must have fallen off the other night. It's flattened. I don't think you can do much with it."

"Thanks," she said as she took it from my hand. Her cell phone rang. When she answered, she paled, said, "Yes. . .yes," then hung up.

"That was the state police. They're coming to get me to take me down for more questioning." She took a shuddering breath. "I don't know if I'm going to survive this."

I wanted to take Abbie's place and face down Detective Reid, but I knew I couldn't.

"This makes me all the more determined to find out who killed Philip," I said. "I've waited a long time for you to be happy. You *are* going to get married in a little over two weeks."

When I picked up Chris from the sitter, he didn't want to leave. I had mixed emotions about that, which, given my desire to go back to work, was amusing. The mother ego part of me wanted him to be clingy. The other part of me was relieved that he was happy with Gladys. That meant I was free to pursue a new job after I solved Philip's murder.

Gladys laughed as she handed my grumpy son to me, wrapped up in his coat. "He's a cute one. And such a good boy."

For everyone but his family, it seems, I thought as he drilled his heels into my sides and complained in my ear.

Her smile suddenly died. "Trish, you've got to do something about your mother and Gail. This disagreement of theirs has gone on long enough. It's starting to impact everything, including the church. The phone lines are burning up."

I was surprised by her vehemence. "What can *I* do?"

"Really, it's your responsibility as your mother's daughter to help her. You can start by trying to talk some sense into both of them. This is just not a healthy situation. Not in any way, shape, or form."

I fought resentment a few minutes later as I tucked Chris into his car seat. Gladys's words settled around me like a noose. How was resolving my mother's fight with Gail *my* responsibility? They were both adults. And I doubted I would be able to talk sense into either woman as stubborn as they were.

I picked up Charlie and made it home just in time for Sammie to arrive. I fed everyone snacks and put an exhausted Chris down for a nap. Then I began to prepare dinner. Not exactly from scratch, since I was making spaghetti with bottled sauce and frozen meatballs, but at least I was cooking instead of ordering pizza.

While the sauce simmered, I put water on to boil for the noodles. Then I sat at the table with my notebook.

After reading through what I'd already written, I jotted down "kitty litter" and thought about that. Weird that it would be next to Philip's body. Especially since he was shot from the woods. Where had the litter come from? Had it been on someone's shoes? Philip's? Or someone else's?

I tapped the pen on the paper. The kitty litter was definitely a clue. How, I wasn't sure. But I needed suspects. The one thing Gladys had said that really made sense to me was to look for people who were strangers in town. Clark was one, and he'd definitely been exposed to kitty litter because of the busted bags he'd delivered to the Adlers' store.

Then there were the Adlers, who had hated Philip for years.

Kitty litter. I frowned. The water for my spaghetti began to boil. I jumped up from the table and put noodles in the pot. As I stirred the sauce, I watched the pasta turning over and over in the water. That's how my brain felt. Like my thoughts were tangled, churning spaghetti noodles. I hoped I could think straight quickly enough to solve this mystery before my best friend's wedding date.

⁓

Chris had more sauce from his chopped-up spaghetti on his mouth than in it. Max smiled at him, and he grinned back. "Dadadadadada."

"He's happy tonight," Max said as if that had never occurred before.

"I think he likes the babysitter," I said. "He didn't want to leave."

Charlie was pushing his spaghetti around on his plate, for once not stuffing his face so fast that remnants landed on his chin.

"Are you feeling okay, honey?" I asked. I was trying to be as normal as possible for my family.

His face squished into a terrible frown. "When is Aunt Abbie going to jail?"

Sammie's mouth dropped open, and she turned to Charlie, big blue eyes filling with tears. "Aunt Abbie is going to jail?"

Charlie nodded solemnly. "I heard in school she killed her husband."

"But Aunt Abbie doesn't have a husband yet," Sammie said. "Did she kill Uncle Eric?"

I glanced desperately at Max. We'd foolishly put off telling the little kids about Abbie, thinking the news wouldn't spread that fast. I didn't know how to tell them. I was afraid I'd cry, and I didn't want them to know how upset I was.

"Aunt Abbie didn't kill anyone," Max said. "Yesterday, Aunt Abbie's ex-husband, Philip, was killed. That's all."

"Yeah, but I heard that she shot him—"

"She didn't," Max told Charlie firmly. "You know your aunt Abbie wouldn't do anything like that."

Sammie looked at me for confirmation. "It's true." I forced myself to smile. "Aunt Abbie didn't shoot anyone. Now I have a great idea. Do you guys remember that cornfield maze we went to last year?"

The kids' expressions immediately brightened.

"I thought maybe we could go this weekend." I glanced at Max. "Friday night?"

He nodded. "Excellent idea. We'll do the maze, take a hay ride, eat s'mores, and drink hot chocolate."

Maybe by then, Philip's murder would be solved. I could only hope.

After dinner, I gave Abbie a quick call to make sure she had survived her time at the state police barracks. She was as good as could be expected. She said that Eric was on his way to her house. He'd read her e-mail, and everything was okay; I knew she'd be in good hands. She also told me that she had spoken with June, who said she'd be delighted to meet with me. After Abbie gave me June's phone number, we exchanged "I love you's" and hung up.

Max and I went to the living room while Sammie and Charlie cleared the table and cleaned the kitchen. Chris was in his high chair in the kitchen with the kids, so Max and I could have a few moments of alone time.

"That was a good meal." He sat on the sofa, and I dropped down next to him. "And a good idea about the cornfield maze. The kids will love it."

"I think we all will."

"How is Abbie?" he asked. "Does she need a lawyer?"

"I'm afraid she's going to." I told him about my visit and how she'd been called to the state police barracks.

"It's not unusual in a case like this that she would be questioned over and over again, especially given what you've told me." He took my hand. "You're still investigating this?"

"Yes, I am. But I do have some news that might make you feel better about it. Corporal Fletcher is working with me to find out more about Philip's murder."

"Oh?" Max's surprise was evident by his raised brows. "That's a little. . .irregular, isn't it? Like, against the rules?"

I smiled at his choice of words. "Yes, it is irregular. He could get in trouble if someone knew. I'm the only one who knows. And now you know, but he made me promise we wouldn't say a word."

"I certainly won't," Max said. "This means you're just collecting clues, right? He'll handle the tough stuff?"

"Yes." I wasn't sure what Max meant by "the tough stuff," but agreeing with his summation was the easiest thing to do.

He bent down to kiss me, which is normally one of my very favorite activities, but because I was too distracted to indulge tonight, I didn't encourage him.

He lifted his head. "I guess that means you're not done talking?"

"No," I said.

He sighed. "Okay."

"Do you remember Ma's neighbor Gladys?"

"You mean the one whose shed you almost burned down when you were eight and decided you needed to learn how to smoke?"

I slapped his arm. "Don't remind me of my past. I wasn't always a good kid."

"Wasn't *always* a good kid?" he asked. "How about *hardly ever*? Your middle name was Trouble."

At my frown, he laughed. "It's true. And you can't say you're not glad our kids aren't like you."

"Well, that's true. I am glad." I couldn't imagine being mother to a child like I had been. But then, my parents were a little odd. Ma always sniped at me, and my daddy spoiled me rotten. I was blessed to have grown up semi-normal, although I was still prone to personality issues that I was trying to work on with God's help. Like selfishness.

"So what about Gladys?" Max asked.

"I think I'm going to leave Chris there when I go back to work part-time."

Max's smile died. "I didn't know your working was a done deal. We haven't really discussed it."

"Yes, we have." I leaned against his shoulder. "Remember? I told you I want to work at Cunningham and Son."

He shook his head. "I was hoping you wouldn't mention that again. I just don't think it's a good idea."

"Well, we worked together at Self-Storage."

He sighed. "Yes, but I was only there sometimes while we were building the other facilities." He paused and squeezed my hand. "I'm worried about it affecting our relationship."

I sat up straight. "But we get along well. . .okay, most of the time."

He stared at me. "I'm just not sure we'd get along working together and living together."

"Does that mean I'm quarrelsome?"

He sighed. "I'm not sure I can explain it right now. Besides, my father wants me to consider a new partner."

"I wanted to be your new partner," I said.

Max avoided my eyes. "Dad has several people in mind. My mother is pushing one in particular, and he doesn't want to battle her."

"Your dad is basically retired, isn't he? How can he make suggestions like that?"

"He's still on the board of directors. And he's still my adviser."

I pulled my hand from his. "So a new partner would be someone who isn't family?"

"Yes. You know who he is. Leighton Whitmore."

"Leighton Whitmore?"

"Yes. I'm not sure about him. I'm still looking into his background and experience." He stared at the wall over my head for a moment, then looked back at me. "I'm sorry."

Irritation slapped at me like an ocean wave. "You know I'm good at what I do, Max. Accounting. Running an office. And I was great with the customers at Four Oaks Self-Storage. It's not like I'm a loose cannon or something. And I care for the company. A stranger would never care like I do."

Max stroked a piece of hair out of my face. "Honey, think about your talents. You have all sorts of options."

He was using his soothing voice. The one he used with the children when they were unreasonable.

I scooted away from him. "And what would those talents be? Why don't you tell me since you're such a know-it-all? Do you mean doing laundry, cooking dinner, and taking care of the children?"

"You know I don't mean that," he said. "Although all of those are commendable qualities and nothing to be ashamed of."

I took a deep breath and tried to regain my composure, but I couldn't. Too many emotions and conflicts warred in me, and worry about Abbie was top on the list.

I jumped to my feet. "I need to go take a bath now."

"Trish. . ." Max reached out a placating hand.

"It's fine. We can talk later. Seriously. I don't want to quarrel."

To his credit, he just let me go. I knew I was being unfair by walking out, but I didn't want to chance a fight. I felt ready to snap.

As I stepped into the tub, Gladys's last words about my mother crept back into my mind, and once again, I felt the responsibility hanging on me. That made me angry. Why was it my responsibility to fix the problem between Ma and Gail? What could I do, really?

And then there was my mother-in-law, Angelica. Our relationship had been strained since the day I met her. Her digs at me hurt. She'd made it very clear I wasn't the ideal daughter-in-law. I had responded by shutting her out of my life and, to a degree, out of the kids' lives. I had a feeling that God was dealing with me about my relationship with Angelica. The problem was, I didn't want to listen.

I deliberately turned my mind to other things, and in just a few minutes, the heat of the bathwater began to loosen the tension in my muscles. I let my brain run on autopilot. I thought about Abbie, Philip, the Adlers, Clark, kitty litter, and Cunningham and Son. How could Max be thinking about hiring someone like Leighton? He wasn't family. He wasn't even from around here. They'd just moved here from. . . I sat up abruptly, splashing the floor with water. Leighton and Hayley had lived in New York City. They were new in town. He was a hunter and owned rifles. And they had kitty litter.

What connection would they have with Philip? Or did I just want them to be guilty of something because the Cunninghams thought they were so perfect?

It was Thursday morning—two weeks and two days before Abbie's wedding. Once again, I'd slept fitfully. While the kids got ready for school, I sat at the table in the kitchen and perused my clue notebook.

Under "Suspects," I quickly jotted down "Hayley and Leighton Whitmore" before I could lecture myself about being biased. Instead, I told myself that a good sleuth follows up all possible leads, no matter what.

When Max walked into the kitchen in a classic gray suit, I murmured hello but kept my eyes on my words. I was still slightly irritated with him.

He bent over to kiss my temple. "I'm sorry about last night. I've given it a lot of thought, and I might have a job idea for you. Just let me think a little bit more, okay?"

I glanced up at him in surprise. "Really? At Cunningham and Son?"

"Yes and no." He grinned. "I'm not going to say anything else right now, so don't ask."

He disappeared through the door to the garage. I felt humbled. Even though Max wanted me home full-time, he loved me enough to want me to be happy. Self-reproach knocked aside my self-righteous crankiness. Max loved me. Enough to allow me to be happy, despite what he wanted. Love sometimes means making choices we don't want to make for the sake of someone else. Doing things we don't want to do. I had a feeling this was a lesson the Lord was trying to teach me. And class wasn't over yet.

Maybe I could hurry my lesson along by trying to help my mother. My first stop after dropping off Chris at the sitter's would be to visit Gail. Maybe I *could* make a difference.

⁓

Gail's house had once stood alone in the middle of ten acres, but as her family grew, she and her husband had subdivided the property, giving each child an acre on which to build a home. That said something about her that went beyond her weirdness and sniping at me. She was loyal to the people she loved, and they returned that loyalty. That was another reason I was surprised by the intensity of the bitterness between her and Ma.

I pulled into the driveway and saw a curtain twitch on one of the front windows. When I got to the door, I rang the bell and waited. Finally, Gail opened the door just enough for me to see her.

"What do you want? If your mother sent you, you can tell her to be happy with Linda."

"She didn't send me," I said. "I came on my own."

Gail didn't move; she just stood like a sentry at the door.

"Can I please come in and talk?" I asked.

Her eyes narrowed. "You're sure you're not here because your mother sent you?"

"Yes, I'm sure." I was trying to think of something that would make her open the door to me. And something that would start the conversation without talking directly about her and Ma. "I—I want to talk to you about Linda."

The mention of Linda's name lit a fire in Gail's eyes. I'd said the right thing. She flung the door open and motioned for me to come in.

"Just go to the living room." She nodded to a room to our left where a soap opera played on the television. "You want anything to drink?"

I shook my head. "No, thank you. I won't be long."

I sat on a beige and blue plaid couch. She dropped heavily into a beige recliner. I looked at her more closely, concerned by the lines in her face. Despite her propensity for joining my mother in marathon Trish-sniping sessions, I liked her. Probably because she'd been my mother's faithful friend for longer than I could remember. Loyalty is something I prize.

"Now," she said, "what do you want to know about that tramp?"

"Linda?"

"Certainly. There aren't any other tramps we were talking about, are there?"

"Well, if—"

"Linda's takin' your ma for a ride. I tried to warn her, but she won't listen to me. I don't have the energy to deal with it right now, but I'll tell you what. She said she needs extra money, but I'm not sure. I think the girl wants something."

"Why do you say that?" I asked. "I thought she was pretty nice. A little dense, maybe."

"Well, that shows you what you know," Gail said.

I found comfort in her familiar dig at me.

"Don't let her fool you. Linda Faye went to school with my daughter. I know what she used to do. She acts ignorant and then stabs you in the back."

"I guess I don't know her that well. But people can change."

Gail snorted. "Change? I doubt that. If you dye a zebra, you still have a zebra."

"Yes, I guess that's true. Only God can change a person's heart."

"And He's got His work cut out for Him with people like Linda." Gail's eyes narrowed, and she leaned forward. "I wouldn't be surprised if she killed Philip Grenville. You do know that she slept with him, too, don't you? She hated him."

Surprise rocked my mind. "I had no idea." Philip's transgressions had cut a wider swath through Four Oaks than I had imagined.

"Oh yes. Back when she lived out with her mama."

"Did she tell you that?"

"No. Philip tried to keep it hush-hush, and so did the women he was involved with. And he made the rounds, believe you me. Seducing them with his uniform and badge. Poor Abbie didn't know the half of it."

"Maybe she did," I murmured. "Do you know who any of the other women were besides Linda?"

Gail's face was twisted in anger. "He made passes at my daughter, Terry, too, but he didn't make any headway. I can't remember who else there was."

"So had he been in touch with Linda?"

"Yes. I overheard her tell one of her friends about it. First time at the fall festival. He wanted to meet with her, and that made her mad."

I had already thought it odd that Philip had contacted

Abbie. Now he had made contact with Linda.

"But she's slick." Gail's eyes narrowed again. "Philip came into the shop for coffee, and Linda was as nice as pie to him."

"Maybe that's because she was at work. Or she thought that if she was nice to him, he'd leave her alone?"

Gail snorted. "No. Something's up." She breathed deeply, and her eyes drifted shut.

"Are you okay?" I asked.

Her lids snapped open. "I'm fine. Just tired. It's my daughter. She's having a hard time. Single mom, you know. She lost her job then got another one. She works with kids at the YMCA, but the hours are terrible. I have to drive my grandbaby to school for a while."

A smile flickered briefly over Gail's lips. "She's in the fourth grade, you know, in a private school. No buses. We pay for it."

I nodded. "It's wonderful that you do that."

Gail's face hardened again. "Terry had just started dating someone, and it looked good for her. Met him through the kids she works with. Then Linda came along and stole him."

Ah. Now the truth came out. Gail's real reason for disliking Linda. "So she took your daughter's boyfriend? Who was it?"

Gail huffed. "Clark Matthews. And then your ma has the nerve to hire Linda after she did that. I can't believe it."

Clark's name kept popping up. And he was beginning to sound like the proverbial Lothario. This also began to explain the rift between Ma and Gail. "Well, why *did* Ma hire Linda? Did she know about all that?"

"No, but she should have had more sense." Gail huffed. "I told her after she hired her, but she said she needed the help 'cause I wasn't there." She took a deep breath. "Now why didn't she just fire Linda?"

I understood how Gail felt. But I knew that my mother couldn't just fire someone based on Gail's grudge. Was it possible this situation might not have a good ending?

"You two have been friends for so long," I said.

"That's my point," she said. "I'm her friend. And she chose someone else." She blinked rapidly, and for just a minute, I saw the real emotion behind the anger. Hurt. And I thought she might cry.

"I'm sorry it's turned out this way," I said. "I know Ma misses you."

Gail recovered and snorted again. "If she missed me, she would get rid of that hussy."

⁓

Although I'd failed in my mission to mend the rift between Gail and my mother, I had tried. I'd learned a few more interesting facts for my clue notebook. And I hoped my talk with Philip's mother, June, would be as enlightening.

On my way to her house, I called Sherry to update her like I'd promised. She didn't answer, so I left her a message telling her what I could and explaining I'd be busy most of the day. I wasn't keen about talking to her, so I hoped she wouldn't call back. I was walking a fine line trying to keep the things secret that needed to be kept secret.

June Grenville lived alone in a neat, long ranch home in a tiny town about twenty miles from me. She'd lived there for years. Nothing had changed since I'd last been here. That was when Abbie and Philip were married.

I took a deep breath and walked to the front porch, which was surrounded by tidy square flower beds and neatly trimmed evergreen shrubs.

The door opened shortly after I knocked. I was surprised. June didn't look a day older than the last time I'd seen her, despite the grief etched on her face. Her hair was a little bit different. Not as long. Now it hung in a pale blond pageboy.

"Trish, how nice to see you. Please come in." She opened the door wide.

I walked past her into a tiled foyer, then I turned to face her. "Thank you for seeing me. I know this is a bad time."

"Bad time. Yes. . .and no."

That was a strange statement. I must have frowned.

"I'll explain in a few minutes," she said with a tiny smile that revealed laugh lines around her eyes. "Please come and sit down. Can I get you anything?"

"No, thank you," I said.

She took me to her living room in the front of the house where modern furniture and glass-topped tables adorned a celery-colored carpet.

I sat on the couch, and she sat across from me in a chair.

"So what can I do for you?" she asked. "Abbie indicated that you wanted to talk to me, but she didn't say why, except that it had to do with Philip."

"Abbie didn't tell you anything?" I asked.

"Just that the police questioned her regarding Philip's death."

"She didn't do it," I blurted out defensively.

June held up a hand. "I don't believe for a minute that Abbie did it." She rubbed her temple. "The police have been here talking to me. I know Abbie understated the issue to me. They kept asking me about her relationship with Philip. Past and present. Like they think she might have done it."

"She's probably considered a suspect." I knew that was as close as I could come to telling her the truth without compromising my promise to Corporal Fletcher.

June leaned forward with an intense gaze. "So why are you here?"

Trying to explain my penchant for sleuthing was hard enough with my family. Explaining it to a relative stranger made me feel weird and maybe a bit presumptuous. "Well, I'm afraid she's going to be arrested, so I'm. . .well, I guess I'm investigating."

June's eyes widened. "Really? Trying to solve my son's. . .murder?"

"Um. . .yes," I said.

"Well now, that's fascinating. Why would you do that? Don't you think the police can handle the investigation?"

I shrugged. "If it was Eric leading the investigation, yes. But this detective seems to have it in for Abbie." I paused and considered my next words. "I could be wrong about it. Maybe it's just the detective's personality, but I want to look into it myself. I can find out things I know the cops can't. And I have a way to get what I discover back to the police."

"Good," she said. "I must admit that Detective Reid's visits here haven't been the best experience for me, and I'm

Philip's mother. She's not a nice person. The worst thing is, I expect she'll be back." June gazed at me with eyes that burned with emotion. I could tell she was trying to figure out what made me tick. "So what makes you think you can solve this? You don't have any police background, do you?"

"If you count being involved in two other murder investigations, then yes." I told her about Jim Bob and Georgia Winters. I also explained that Max wasn't thrilled with what I was doing.

"I should think not," June said. "But I can see you're determined. And I want to see Abbie cleared as much as you do." I squirmed under June's steady, assessing gaze. Then I saw the change in her eyes when she made up her mind. "I believe you might be able to do this."

Her expression of confidence made me feel better, but I was still confused by her emotional state. She wasn't behaving at all like I would expect a grieving mother to act. "So you do believe Philip was murdered—that it wasn't just an unfortunate accident?"

"Don't you?" she asked. "What is the likelihood that he was shot with a stray bullet from a hunter's rifle? In an area posted No Hunting? In that location near the church?"

I nodded. "I feel exactly like you do, which is why I'm here. The police don't appreciate my help, by the way."

"I don't imagine they do." She stood and walked to a side table that was covered with framed pictures. She picked up two and held them out to me. I took the first from her hand. It was Abbie and Philip at their wedding. I had a similar picture in an album at home.

I glanced up at June to ask why she'd shown me the

photo, but the two tiny trickles of tears running down her cheeks stopped me. At last. Signs of mourning.

"I'm sorry," I said. "I feel insensitive."

She sniffed. "It's fine, Trish, really. Please ignore my tears. I just want you to know that the day Abbie married Philip, she became like another daughter to me. That hasn't changed." She handed the next picture to me. This one was a family shot of her, Philip, and a younger woman.

"Is that your daughter?"

June nodded. "Mary. This was taken a few years ago during one of his brief visits here."

If body language in the picture was any indication of relationships, Mary and Philip didn't get along well. He had his arm around her shoulders, but they were stiff. I could have put a fist between their bodies. "How often did Philip visit?"

"Regularly and on holidays."

That meant Philip was in town many times without contacting Abbie.

"Mary will be here tomorrow. We're going to bury Philip Sunday afternoon in a private service. Then she's going to stay with me for a while." She took the pictures from me. Tears still flowed down her cheeks. Ignoring her obvious pain was difficult. While her initial lack of expression had been puzzling, this was much worse. I wanted to either hold her in my arms or leave so she could be alone. I could only imagine the grief of losing a child. I took a deep breath and steeled myself for the questions I had to ask.

"I guess I was always a little surprised that you weren't angry at Abbie for the end of the marriage."

"How could I be? We all knew how Philip was changing for the worse." She placed the picture back on the table and stroked the glass. "He wasn't always like that, you know. Something changed. It might have been his work—I don't know. Or his father's death. But Philip got worse after he married Abbie. It was like the responsibility of marriage brought out the worst in him." She turned around and gazed at me. "I always suspected that he hurt her."

I said nothing. I didn't know if Abbie wanted anyone to know.

June's glance was sharp. "You don't have to say anything. I know. I just wish I'd had the courage back then to step in. Maybe things would have been different—"

"I think we all have regrets," I said.

She dropped back into her chair and visibly drew herself back together. "How will you proceed?"

"First, I want to figure out why Philip came back after all this time. Why he wanted to talk to Abbie so badly."

"Oh, I can tell you that."

I almost fell out of my chair. I was finally going to get an answer to my question, and so easily.

June fingered the edge of her shirt. "Most people didn't know that he came back on a regular basis to visit since he made sure no one knew he was here. He was never successful in his relationships, but he did take care of me. Too many people around here didn't like him. But this time was different. He. . ."

I waited for her to finish. Her mouth worked; it was obvious that what she had to say was painful. Then she met my gaze with her tear-filled eyes. "He was dying. He had just months to live. Cancer."

I felt my mouth drop open. Of everything I might have thought June would tell me, I never would have guessed that in a million years.

The corner of her mouth twitched, despite her pain. "You're shocked. I understand. When I first found out, I couldn't believe it. But hang on for what I have to say next." Her smile grew, although she was still crying. "It was a mixed blessing. Because of his illness, he finally decided to go to church. He committed his life to the Lord. That's why he moved back here. He had a lot of things here he felt he'd left undone. People he'd hurt. And he wanted to make everything right."

I felt like the floor had dropped out from under me. Philip Grenville? He'd *moved* back here? And he was in a relationship with God?

"I'm sorry," I said. "I don't know what to say."

"I understand. It took me awhile to believe it. While he was sick, I went to see him. I wasn't sure I believed him. He was always such a good manipulator, even though Mary assured me it was true. I have to tell you, I was still skeptical when he walked in here two weeks ago with a suitcase in one hand and a Bible in the other." She clasped her hands tightly. "I feel terrible, really. Here he was dying, and I was suspicious that he was just being the same old Philip. Somehow being manipulative because he wanted something. Or poking fun at my religion. His own mother didn't believe him. Then he started to talk to me about what had happened." She smiled despite teary eyes. "Can you imagine?"

"No. I can't." Something shifted in my head, making me think beyond my shock of Philip's transformation.

"He came here two weeks ago?"

June reached for a tissue from a box on her coffee table and wiped her cheeks and nose. "Yes. He'd spent brutal months in treatment. Then the cancer returned, so he came here to die. He didn't go to a doctor again, except once to Dr. Starling for an unrelated illness."

June picked up a pillow and hugged it. "His sister, Mary, was with him for his last few weeks of treatment. I had to work and couldn't get the time off."

"I'm glad he had someone there with him," I mumbled. I was still trying to wrap my mind around everything June had said.

She nodded. "I was, too. And I think you'll need to talk to Mary, as well, after she's had a couple of days to settle in. She recently experienced a bad real estate deal in Atlanta and lost some money, so she needs to get financially stable again. At least that's her excuse for moving in with me. I know she really wants to make sure I'm okay.

"Anyway, she was as shocked as I was at his change. When the treatments were over, she went back home. Then we got the news that the cancer had returned. The doctors told him he should get his affairs in order."

"But. . .how. . ."

"How did he have such a change of heart?" she asked.

I nodded.

"He had a fellow officer who had been witnessing to him for years." She paused and wiped her eyes. "When a person comes face-to-face with their own mortality and sees imminent death, it changes their perspective."

I nodded.

"I've prayed for him and the people he hurt for years,"

June said. "He was a manipulative, selfish man. I still loved him as a son, but I saw the trail of misery he left behind him. That was difficult. His change of heart was certainly an answer to my prayers, but I had to work through a surprising evolution of feelings before I could believe him and accept what had happened. Then when he was shot, I once again had to sort through mixed emotions."

I waited for her to explain.

"The cancer diagnosis was tragic," she said, "but it led to his salvation. His murder was tragic, but it did save him from the suffering he would have eventually endured from his illness. I wish I'd had the extra month or two with him, but the little time we did have was perfect. . .so you can see why I feel the way I do."

"Yes." The tangled spaghetti that was my brain was having trouble taking all of this in. "So. . .that's why he was pursuing Abbie."

June squeezed the pillow. "Yes. He wanted to make things right. He knew what he had done to her. He told me that she wouldn't talk to him. Not that I blame her, mind you. He probably came on too strong." She smiled briefly. "Just because someone gets saved doesn't mean they have a personality transplant. But I was going to intervene and call her that night and ask her to see him."

"Were you aware of a letter he sent to her?"

"Yes," June said. "He wrote that right before he left New York City. He wanted to get together with her once he'd settled in here. But she returned it without opening it." I watched June's face for any anger, but there didn't seem to be any. She noticed my perusal. "I can't blame Abbie for her reaction. And he didn't, either." Anger suddenly flashed in her eyes. "That detective took the letter away. I was stupid. I was in such a state of shock after I was told he'd been shot that I just gave them blanket permission to go through his belongings. I should have insisted on a warrant and taken the time to get what I wanted. Now they're using it against Abbie, I'm sure."

"You didn't know," I said. "How could you?"

June took a deep breath. "Yes, you're right, of course, but I still blame myself."

"Abbie is going to blame herself, too," I murmured, "for not giving him a chance."

"He understood." When June leaned back and her body seemed to collapse in on itself, I realized our talk had worn her out. I had three final things to ask.

"Did you go with Philip to the fall festival?"

June shook her head. "No. I had to work that day, so he dropped me off at my job and then he went out there to see if he could talk to Abbie."

"Did he say anything about being there? Anything unusual? Like maybe about someone he'd seen besides Abbie?"

June pursed her lips and frowned. "You know what? He was acting funny. He didn't say anything—that I remember. But he was a bit late picking me up. And he was distracted. I thought at first he and Abbie had quarreled, but he said no."

"Well, if you think of anything else about that, let me know, okay?"

She agreed.

I sat forward and put my arms on my legs. "Did Philip have any signs of having been in a fight with someone?"

She sighed. "You mean that black eye?"

I nodded.

"He got that last Sunday. We ate lunch after church, and then he took the car out for a while. When he got back, he had that shiner, but he refused to tell me what happened."

"Do you know Jaylene and Henry Adler?" I asked.

June frowned. "Vaguely. I've heard the name. Pet store?"

"Yes."

"Why?" she asked.

"Because they hated Philip for some reason." I stared at my hands before looking up at her. "I really appreciate your time. You've been more help than you realize."

"You're welcome. I want to make things as right as they can possibly be for Abbie." June smiled again. "Philip would have wanted it that way."

I stood. "I'll leave you now. If you think of anything else, would you call me?"

She stood up, as well. "Yes. And I'll tell Mary that she needs to speak with you."

We walked to the front door. "Trish?"

I faced her.

"Will you tell Abbie what I told you? I think it might be better coming from you. Well, at least easier right now. I—I think this will take some adjustment for her. And it will be easier if she doesn't have to see me while she's figuring things out."

"Yes, I'll tell her."

June touched my arm. "When she's ready to hear it, please tell her this. Philip was happy she was successful. He wanted to tell her that he couldn't think of anybody better than Eric Scott to take care of her."

I walked to my SUV feeling overwhelmed by the information I'd just learned. Philip had not died the bad
man I thought he was. Although I was relieved, now I
wondered how to deal with all the anger and resentment
I felt toward him. At first glance it might seem simple.
He'd changed. He was trying to make things right. God
had forgiven him; therefore, I should. But feelings can't be
eradicated that easily.

I thought about the song "Amazing Grace" and
realized that though I'd sung it in church all my life, I'd
never grasped the depth of the simple truth. God can walk
into someone's life and so totally transform them that they
aren't the same person they were before. Even someone
who has hurt other people so badly.

The Bible says that God leaves the past behind. I
couldn't do that so easily. How odd to be in the position
of having to forgive a dead man. That might take some
time. But I did feel an odd sense of relief. If a tragic death
can have a good side, Philip's did.

And now I had to prepare myself to tell Abbie what
I'd found out—why Philip had been so insistent about
talking to her. And I would have to watch her go through
the same emotional processes I was going through, only
magnified hundreds of times.

Given her already fragile emotional state, I had a
feeling she would take her response to what I told her and
add it to the heaps of guilt she was already carrying. But I

hoped that gradually she would be able to come to peace with his death. And take the gift God offered her through Philip's change of heart—freedom from the past. And his wish that she would be happy with Eric.

Lord, please give me the right words.

I shivered from the cold, stuck my keys in the ignition, and turned on my SUV, but I didn't go anywhere. Instead, I blindly stared at June's house, trying to think of the best way to handle this. Maybe I should ask Abbie to meet me somewhere for lunch so I could tell her in a neutral place. If she was in public, she might not retreat so quickly into herself.

I dug through all the junk in my purse for my cell phone. As I called her, I made a mental note to clean the mess.

"How are you?" I asked when she answered.

"Hanging in there." She sounded livelier than she had that last time I spoke with her.

"Anything new?" I asked.

"No. I spent some good time with Eric. He just left."

"I'm glad," I said. "Listen, can you meet me for lunch?"

I heard her inhale. "Today? I don't really want to go out in public right now. I hate it when people stare at me."

"Let's go somewhere out of town. Where no one will notice us." I thought about it. "You know that really great Italian place near Angelica's? It'll be my treat."

"I don't know. . . ."

"Abbie, you need to get out." How could I convince her? "But more than that, there's something I have to tell you."

"Something you *have* to tell me?"

"Yes. About Philip. Please."

"About Philip." She paused. "You just talked to June, didn't you?"

"Yes."

Abbie didn't say anything for a moment, and I flicked my keys with my finger, making them jingle.

"I won't be able to convince you to tell me on the phone, will I?" she asked. "Or to come over here?"

"No," I said.

She sighed. "Okay. I know you wouldn't ask me if you didn't think it was important."

"Oh, Abs?" I said quickly before she hung up. "Would you please bring a blank bookplate with you? I need an autograph for someone."

⁓

I arrived at the restaurant before Abbie and got a table right away. After I slipped into my chair and put my sunglasses on the table, I pulled my steno pad from my purse to make notes. I hadn't felt right making notes while I was talking to June, but I needed to do so now before I forgot anything.

I wrote a small paragraph about Philip's transformation—something I was still having trouble wrapping my mind around. Then I began adding specific clues.

> *Philip making amends. Had he approached someone with a real grudge? A grudge big enough to kill him?*

To my last notation about Philip leaving the fall

festival abruptly, I added:

> *He was distracted—maybe disturbed by*
> *someone or something. What? And he'd been in*
> *town for a couple of weeks.*
> *He got the black eye the Sunday after the fall*
> *festival. He went somewhere alone after church.*

Then I tapped my pen against my lip. After talking to Gail, I had another potential suspect for my list. Linda Faye King.

I wrote:

> *Linda. Possibly slept with Philip long ago.*
> *She was trying to avoid him now. Was she angry*
> *enough about the past to kill him now? Or possibly*
> *afraid of him for some reason?*

Something niggled in my mind. The fall festival seemed to be the one place where all my suspects and Philip had been at the same time.

Clark, Linda, the Adlers. . .Hayley and Leighton. I paused my mental rundown of suspects and bit the end of my pen. What about Gail and her daughter? Though I hated to think about it, there was definitely some hostility there. Just to be thorough, I jotted down "Gail."

My quest for information would continue that afternoon. I'd drop by Clark's mother's after lunch with the bookplate.

And maybe it was time to look for houses—a good excuse to see Linda. I yanked out my cell and gave her a quick call at her office. She was in, and we agreed to a meeting on Saturday afternoon when we could discuss what I had in mind.

I put away my phone. And looked at the names on my list. I needed to find out more about Hayley and Leighton. Sammie and I would go visit the kitten again. But I'd give Angelica a call a bit later and try to pry some information out of her.

I was concentrating so hard, I didn't notice Abbie until she joined me at the table. I shut my notebook and put it away. She kissed my cheek then slipped into her seat and pulled a bookplate out of her purse. "Who is this for?"

"Clark Matthews' mother, Eunice."

She wrote on the plate and then handed it to me. "So is there a reason for this?"

I tucked the plate into my purse and met her gaze. "Yes. I'm trying to find a killer."

"Still hard at work on my behalf," she said.

"Yes."

"Thank you." She clasped her hands on the table. "I don't deserve the kind of friend you are to me. And I don't deserve Eric, either. Not after the way I've kept things from him."

"Don't be silly." I reached across the table and squeezed her hands. "You've put up with so many of my faults."

"No more than you put up with mine." She smiled. "Hey, how many people have a best friend—a true best friend? And you've been mine since before kindergarten."

We touched the tips of our index fingers, something that had been a sign of our friendship for years. When we were little, we decided we wanted to be blood sisters. We'd pricked the ends of our fingers to make them bleed and then held them together. Strangely enough, that childish action meant more today than it had then. It represented the covenant of our friendship.

We were both silent for a few minutes after that. My mind was filled with a montage of memories. Finally, Abbie broke the silence.

"Eric suspects that Nick Fletcher is investigating Philip's murder on his own time."

I tried hard to look innocent, but she'd caught me off guard, and I was sure my face gave me away.

"You knew, didn't you?" she asked.

I stared at the tablecloth. "I can't say."

The corners of her mouth twitched. "I understand. Eric says he can't officially know what Nick is doing because he'd have to order him to stop, so he hasn't told Nick he knows. However, during one of their conversations, Eric mentioned offhand to him the name of someone at the state police who might be able to feed him a bit of information, and vice versa."

I glanced down at the table to cover up my surprise. While I was glad for what Eric was doing, I was pretty sure Abbie didn't understand the implications. Eric was a letter-of-the-law kind of guy. Black-and-white. For him to be encouraging Corporal Fletcher to step outside the system, even in such a subtle way, told me just how frightened Eric really was for Abbie.

"So what did you want to talk to me about?" Abbie asked.

No getting around it. Things were getting more complicated by the minute.

"Why don't we order," I said. "Then I'll tell you everything."

We didn't have to wait long for our server. I ordered the Tuscan chicken; Abbie ordered lasagna.

"Are you really going to eat?" I asked.

"I'm going to try," she said. "Talking to Eric helped." She smiled softly. "He understands why I kept things from him. All in all, I'm feeling a bit more upbeat."

"I'm so glad." I wished with all my heart that I wasn't about to shatter her good feelings into a million pieces.

I began by telling her how June had looked. How well she was doing despite everything. How pretty the house was. How nicely June had kept things up.

Abbie put a finger in the air in front of my mouth. "You're avoiding telling me something, aren't you?"

I sighed. "Yes."

The muscles in her face tightened. "That means I should brace myself." She sat up and straightened her shoulders.

I took a deep breath. Then I blurted out everything. As I spoke, a gamut of emotions washed over her face. Several times, I could tell she was on the verge of tears.

"That's it," I said when I was finished.

"That's it?" She swallowed hard.

"Yes, that's it." I'd done the right thing by bringing her here. Abbie would not fall apart in public, and I needed time to get through to her.

I watched her jaw clench and relax and clench and relax, as if she were chewing gum. I knew the signs. She was about to let loose.

"So because I was afraid of Philip and angry at him,

he wasn't allowed the satisfaction of asking my forgiveness. That's selfish of me, isn't it?"

I was right about her blaming herself. "It's not that simple," I said. "You can't—"

"But it's worse than that. Not only did I *not* allow him to talk to me but I'm still terribly angry at him. How's that for ironic? I'm angry at a dead man. That's really selfish."

"I understand. That's how I—"

"And now"—she slapped her hands on the table—"even dead, he's making my life miserable. He had the nerve to die in the middle of my wedding plans. And I'm mad about that. How's that for selfish?"

"Well, you—"

"And to top it all off, I'm a suspect. Is this right? Is this fair? He makes everyone's lives miserable for years, then he comes riding into town like some kind of heroic, dying, movie-hero cowboy, ready to fix everything. And he wants the woman he left behind *plus* all the townspeople to forgive him. Just like that." She snapped her finger.

"I'm not sure he was expecting—"

"Then he ups and gets shot by a bad guy and doesn't even have to follow through on his plans. And he dies and goes to heaven, leaving the rest of us here to pick up all the pieces and try to put things back together."

"That's probably—"

"And the worst thing is that I'm a Christian. I'm supposed to be rejoicing that he turned to the Lord at the end of his life. Rejoicing that he was delivered from the fires of hell." She glared at me. "I'm glad he didn't go to hell, but I am not rejoicing. I'm just plain mad."

Abbie had a way with words. Considering she was a

writer, that was to be expected. She'd managed to express some of what I'd been thinking, only better. And she summed it up quite nicely.

I waited to see if she was done. She appeared to be. She was breathing hard, and her face was flushed. Truthfully, I was glad to see her feisty and angry instead of morose and depressed.

"Well. . ." I paused long enough to give her a chance to interrupt me. She didn't. That meant her tirade was over. "You've probably just expressed some of what I was feeling, too."

Abbie finally noticed I was speaking and stared at me with wide eyes. "You mean you don't think I'm horrible for thinking all of that?"

I shook my head. "Absolutely not. I'm having some pretty deep issues of my own about this."

"Really?"

"You'd better believe it." I leaned toward her. "So did June at first, and she's his mother. I think she suspected you'd feel all of this, which is why she didn't want to tell you herself."

Abbie blinked as tears filled her eyes again. "I'm a wreck. A total emotional basket case. I go from one emotion to the other in a matter of seconds."

"I know," I said. "Do you want me to tell Eric?"

"No. I'll tell him." She pulled another tissue from her purse.

Our food arrived, and Abbie turned her head so the server wouldn't notice her tears. After the server left, I reached over and patted Abbie's arm.

"I'm so sorry. I knew this would be hard. Will you be able to eat?"

She blew her nose and smiled valiantly. "How could I waste the best lasagna on the East Coast? I'm going to try."

She managed to eat half her meal, and I did the same. To give her time to recover, I did most of the talking—about the kids and Max. I told her I wanted to go back to work.

"That doesn't surprise me," she said. "You've never been able to be at home and settle. Even when you were a kid."

We chatted about a few more things and avoided the topic of Philip altogether. When we were done, I paid our bill and we both stood. I pulled her into a tight hug.

"I love you. This will work out. You wait and see."

"I want to believe that," she said.

So did I.

"Oh," said Abbie, reaching into her purse. "I forgot to give you this." She pulled the smashed button I'd found in the parking lot from her pocket. "This isn't mine."

I took it from her and dropped it into my purse. Perhaps it just belonged to a church member.

We exchanged good-byes, and I watched her leave, shoulders slumped. I ached for her.

I went to the bathroom before I left. That's when I realized I'd left my sunglasses on the table. I went back to get them and noticed a couple walking into another room of the restaurant. I would recognize Linda anywhere. I also recognized the man with her. Leighton Whitmore. Hayley's husband! Why were they together?

And that's when I remembered there were two other people who'd had gold buttons on their clothing on the day of Philip's murder.

Linda Faye King and Hayley Whitmore.

—

I'd brought my headset with me that day, so I was free to make all the calls I needed to as I drove.

First, I called Clark's mother, Eunice Matthews, to ask if I could come by and deliver her bookplate. She seemed eager for the visit and explained how to get to her house. Then I called April to see if she wanted to come with me to visit Eunice, but April informed me that she was, like, *way* over Clark and that Linda could have him. But did Linda want Clark? Or did she have her sights on a wealthier man—Leighton Whitmore?

As I drove to Eunice's house, I called Corporal Fletcher. I needed to update him while everything was fresh in my mind.

"Fletcher," he snapped into the receiver.

"This is Trish Cunningham. Is this a good time to talk?"

"Mrs. C." His tone lightened. "I'm on the road, so yeah. You have news for me?"

"I don't know. Maybe."

"Well, just shoot. I'll ask questions if I have them."

I told him everything I'd learned so far. Several times, he grunted. I even mentioned Leighton and Linda. Then I told him about my visit with June and everything we'd talked about, including Philip's change of heart.

"You gotta be kidding me," Fletcher said.

"Kidding?" I asked. "Kidding about what?"

"Philip got religion?"

I could hear the derision in his voice, and I felt defensive for June's sake. "Well, that's what his mother said. And she would know. She *is* his mother."

Fletcher snorted.

"Hey, why so cynical?" I asked. "Why don't you believe it?"

"His mommy said so?" After a bark of laughter, Fletcher sighed. "Sorry, Mrs. C., but you wouldn't believe how many people's mothers cover for them. And how many people claim religious conversion. Or lie to get something. Now, granted, he probably didn't have anything to gain from this, so it's possible. But. . ."

"I'm sorry, too," I said.

"Sorry for what?"

"I'm sorry that you're so cynical. Really, Corporal Fletcher. What a horrible way to live."

He laughed again, and this time it sounded genuine. "That's what I like about you. You tell me exactly what you're thinking." He sighed again. "You're right. About the cynicism. It's my job that does it. I see the bad side of people all the time. You wouldn't believe the stupid stuff people lie about."

"I can imagine." And I really could understand, given my brief foray into crime. Especially since I'd lied one time, too.

"I'll tell you what." He chuckled. "Since Philip is so tragically dead, I'll believe his mommy and give him the benefit of the doubt."

"That's just slightly insensitive," I said primly. "I think it must be a form of cop humor. A lot of people wouldn't find that very funny, you know. Still, I'm glad you can make an exception to the way you usually think and believe a dead man, but don't strain yourself."

That just made him laugh harder, and I joined him.

"You, Mrs. C., are exactly what I needed at the moment. And while we're at it—how about you call me Nick? Seeing as how we're working together and are going to be related by friendship."

I felt warm inside. "That is probably one of the nicest things you've ever said to me. And I'd be honored. You can call me Trish."

"I can try, but I think Mrs. C. suits you better."

I heard his car radio in the background. "Listen, gotta go. And the other things you told me today? Good stuff. Keep me posted, okay? Anything you hear. It might not seem like much, but you never know."

"You got it," I said and clicked my phone off.

How true a statement was that? Sometimes it was the smallest detail, the quirkiest turn of events that led to a killer.

Shortly after, bookplate in hand, I showed up at Eunice Matthews's doublewide.

She must have been waiting for me, because she opened the door before I could knock.

"Trish Cunningham?"

"Yes."

"I'm Eunice. You made it here quickly. Please come in."

The tiny birdlike woman stepped back for me to walk by. Her dark hair was tightly permed and curled close to her scalp. I could see a very faint resemblance to her son in her nose and mouth, but they both looked a lot better on him than they did on her. And she didn't look sick to me, but what did I know?

Inside, I was immediately overwhelmed by the smell of floral air freshener. She pointed to a small living area just next to the foyer. I looked around and felt like I had stepped into a peach-orchard explosion. The couch was a floral peach pattern, the carpet a darker shade of the color. Even the flowers in the large print hanging above the sofa were peach. The only relief came in the little bits of brown and green accent colors and the wood of the other furniture, including a glass case standing in a prominent corner of the room. That was filled with a collection of angels, mostly fat little winged babies—with peach-tinted skin.

I dropped onto the sofa and took the bookplate from my purse. As Eunice passed me and headed for a peach-colored lounge chair, I handed it to her with Abbie's regards.

She took it from my hand and sat with a smile.

"Oh my," she said. "How exciting! This is very thoughtful. Clark told me that he'd asked you for it. He's such a good boy. Always thinking of his mama."

So Clark had told her it was his idea? I eyed my hostess. Her blue cotton pants had a knife-edge crease in them, and the sleeves on her matching blue-checked shirt had the same. She wore white socks and black loafers. Everything about her screamed "neat and tidy."

"He went to that book signing to get me an autographed copy of the book, but he said there was a line and then he had to leave because someone he knew needed help changing a tire." She smiled. "He's such a thoughtful boy. He bought me all this when he was working in New York, you know." She lifted her hand and pointed at everything in the room.

I wondered which of them was the interior designer. Still, I had to admit the decor somehow suited her.

"Well now, look at me. Look at my manners. Let me get you some coffee." She stood and walked to the tidy kitchen where the peach decor was continued in the accents and wall color.

My mind had gone totally blank. I wondered if it was shock, perhaps as a result of the color detonation surrounding me.

"Clark loves my coffee. He thinks it's better than anything, including the coffee at Doris's Doughnuts, and you know everyone loves hers, me included."

I remembered how Clark had complimented my mother's coffee, and I wondered if Eunice knew that I was Doris's daughter. I wasn't sure, and I didn't ask.

She asked me how I wanted my coffee, fixed it for me, and brought it to me. The peach-colored mug said TOMORROW IS ANOTHER DAY on the side.

"Clark gave me these mugs."

I made the appropriate complimentary noises and took a sip of the coffee. It was bad. Like dishwater.

"Good, isn't it?" she asked.

"Mmm," I said so I wouldn't have to lie outright. "So I understand that Clark only recently moved here?"

A smile lit her face. "Yes. I was never so glad in my life. I wanted him to get away from the city. Now he's here to be near me."

She seemed fine to me. "So Clark lived in New York City, then?"

"Oh yes." She took a deep breath and clasped her hands together. "I suppose you've heard what he was doing there."

"You mean. . .modeling work?" I wasn't sure exactly how to say what I'd heard his job was.

"Yes." She beamed. "He was a successful model. Always sending me money."

"Did you, um, see his work?"

She waved a hand. "I've seen some pictures in his portfolio. He said those were the best."

I thought about what Angelica had said a few days ago. Something about how long it takes mothers to see the truth about their children.

"He's settling in nicely," Eunice said. "Making nice friends. Better than some of the people he knew in the city." Her mouth pursed in disapproval. "I know he always adopts people and tries to take care of them. He'd bring them with him to visit me, but I didn't like them."

I murmured something sympathetic to encourage her to talk. Not that she needed much encouragement.

She hopped up from her chair, once again reminding me of a little bird. She snatched a framed picture from a shelf in the corner and held it out to me. Somehow I must have missed it in the peach overload.

"That's one of his best shots."

"Very nice." At last, I was telling the truth, because Clark *did* look good. Classic movie-star kind of looks. In the image of Cary Grant and Clark Gable. I handed the picture to her, and she put it back on the shelf. Then she perched on the edge of her chair again.

"I was so glad he moved here to get away from the city and be near me."

I put my cup on the end table after several brave attempts to drink the coffee. "Well, I'm glad he's living here, too."

"Yes, but I'm worried about him. He's having problems with complaints at work."

"Complaints? What kind of complaints?"

Her chin wiggled in indignation. "He told me about how that nasty woman at the pet store called his boss and complained that he was breaking open bags of cat litter. She probably did it and just blamed him, but he got in trouble."

"Well, I'm sorry to hear that," I said. I thought about how charming Clark had been to Jaylene. It had all been an act.

She shook her head. "I'm sure it couldn't have been as bad as she said, although I did pick cat litter out of the carpet in his bedroom for five minutes."

Cat litter. Again.

Eunice clasped her hands together. "Clark is getting involved quickly in the community. He's taking some classes at the junior college to improve himself. He's gone out hunting with some of the men he met on the job. He's also involved with some activities at the YMCA now. Helping underprivileged youth."

That surprised me. He hadn't hit me as a philanthropic kind of guy. But the thing I was most interested in was the hunting. "Does he have his own guns?"

"Oh my, well, they're his father's. He and his father used to go hunting, so this is like a return to his childhood."

Clark just moved up on my suspect list.

"He also has a very nice girlfriend," his mother said.

I stared at her. "He does?" I waited for what I knew was coming.

"Yes. Very pretty and successful. Her name is Linda."

On Friday morning, I was at loose ends after updating my clue notebook with a few notations about Clark. Like the fact that he hunted and was taking classes. I also noted that he was an actor. Saying whatever the person he was talking to wanted to hear. That wasn't really a clue. Most people do that to a degree.

Sherry called me between classes.

"Hey," I said.

"Dad isn't telling me very much." She sounded so down that I wished she were with me so I could hug her.

"There's not a lot to tell, but things are progressing." I tried to sound cheery.

After a moment of silence, she sighed. "You don't have to fib to make me feel better."

"I'm sorry," I said. "I wish I had more to tell you."

"Can we go over your clues one more time?" she asked.

I obliged her.

"Mrs. C., I know you're trying hard, but this wedding has to happen. My dad hasn't been this happy in a long time. And neither have I. We both need Abbie." Her voice broke.

I felt tears in my eyes along with the weight of my failure so far.

I agreed. We both hung up feeling worse than we had when we started. I looked at my suspect list again. I had to find out more about Hayley and Leighton. I picked up the cell phone and did something I rarely do. I called my mother-in-law.

"Patricia." I could tell by the tone of her voice that she was as surprised to hear from me as I was that I actually called her. "Is something wrong?"

Guilt slapped me. If I needed another indication that she wasn't the only problem in our relationship, that was it.

"Yes, everyone is fine. I have a couple of questions for you."

"Questions?" she asked quickly. "What about?"

"I'm just curious. What do you know about Leighton and Hayley?"

She paused before she answered. "Enough. Hayley is a good friend of mine."

"Well, how long have you known them?"

"For nine months. Since they moved here."

"So you know nothing about them before that?"

"Well, certainly I do. Hayley and I are friends. Patricia, what is this about?"

"I was just wondering."

She didn't say anything, and I knew the wheels in her head were turning. But before I could figure out a good way to distract her, I heard her quick intake of breath. "You're trying to solve the mystery of who killed Philip Grenville, aren't you? Because your friend was arrested."

I had to hand it to her. My mother-in-law might be a snob, but she's a smart one. She is, after all, the mother of the smartest man I know.

"You can't think that Hayley or Leighton had anything to do with this," she said. "They don't even *know* Abbie."

"Yes, well, I saw Leighton with someone who does know Abbie. And Philip. I have to follow up on all the leads."

"Well, I'm sure you're wrong. You're wasting your time."

The frost in Angelica's voice would have discouraged most anyone else, but not me. I had to find out more information. I felt a little prick of conscience and made an impulsive decision.

"Would you like to go with me and Sammie to look at her kitten? Maybe tomorrow, if Hayley is available?"

In the silence after my question, I realized I'd surprised her. That's when I knew I needed to make some changes. It was time to be an adult and try to cross the bridge of hostility and reach out to my mother-in-law. Then it would be her choice to accept me or not.

My offer distracted her from my questions about Leighton. We agreed on a time, and she said she'd check with Hayley and let me know if it wouldn't work. After I hung up, I went to the kitchen and dropped into a chair. My overly stuffed purse sat on the table. I needed a distraction, and a good one was sitting right in front of me.

I dumped the contents on the table, pulled the trash can next to me, and began sorting. Pens from coins. Important receipts from old grocery lists. I was about to drop what looked like an old list into the trash when I realized it wasn't my writing. And I didn't recognize the torn paper.

I laid it on the table in front of me and smoothed it out. The scrawl was strong and looked masculine. And it was only partial:

> *. . .to meet with you. We have to talk. It's important. Can you meet me Sunday afternoon at the store?*

It was the signature that made my heart flip over. *Philip Grenville.*

Sunday afternoon. When Philip got his black eye. Where had this come from? I banged my fist softly against my forehead. Not from Sammie. She never added her collections to my purse, just kept them in her pockets. Store? Then I remembered how Chris had knocked my purse over in Adler's Pet Emporium. Jaylene had scooped up stuff off the floor at her feet. After Henry had riffled through the drawer under the cash register. I'd seen some of the papers from that drawer fall to the floor. Could this letter have come from the Adlers' store?

I didn't have time to think about it because my cell phone rang. I actually remembered to check the caller ID and wished I hadn't because suddenly I wanted to throw up.

"Hello?"

"Mrs. Cunningham, this is Detective Reid."

"Yes?" I asked.

"I wonder if you could come talk to me at the state police barracks, say, in an hour?"

"All right," I said, dread tightening my stomach.

She explained where the barracks were.

I pushed the END button on the phone and picked up the scrap of paper I'd found in my purse. I knew a responsible citizen would give this to Detective Reid. But I didn't like her; therefore, I didn't want to help her. I punched Nick Fletcher's number into my phone.

"Hey, Mrs. C.," he said as a greeting. "I'm in the middle of something. Is this important?"

"Yes." In a rush, I told him about the scrap of paper and going to see the detective.

"Give it to her," he said without hesitation. "It could help Abbie."

His words were like a slap. I was so busy not liking Detective Reid that I'd failed to think of the bigger picture. "Okay. I'll do that."

"Listen, anything could help right now." He took a deep breath. "I gotta tell ya, Mrs. C., things aren't lookin' so good for Abbie right now."

I dropped Chris off at Gladys's house. Corporal Fletcher's last words kept rolling through my mind as I pulled up to the state police barracks. I felt a tremor of nerves as I approached the door.

Inside, I was immediately escorted to a plain white interview room. Unlike the sheriff's office, this room had seen much better days. I was surprised that Detective Reid didn't keep me waiting long. She bustled in, carrying a folder, a pen, and a bottle of water.

"Can I get you anything before we begin?" she asked. "Like some water or a cup of coffee?"

"No, thanks. I just had lunch. But before we begin, I have something to give you." I pulled the scrap of paper from a pocket in my purse and handed it to her.

She glanced at it, her eyes widening as she read it. Then she looked back at me. "Where did you get this?"

I explained everything while she watched me with emotionless eyes.

When I was finished, I said, "I'd just found it when you called me."

"Mmm." She sounded like she didn't believe me, but it was hard to tell, given she always sounded like that. "I'd just like to cover a few additional points today."

"Okay." I sat back to wait for the conversational hail to begin.

She opened the file, slipped the scrap of paper I'd given her inside, and turned to another page. Then she looked up at me.

She tapped a stubby-nailed finger on her notes. "Your mother was overheard to have said something about shooting Philip."

Of all the things I thought Detective Reid would say, that wasn't one of them. My surprise must have been evident on my face. Her eyes narrowed. I wanted to kick myself. One point for her. Zero for me.

"When was that?" I asked, even though I remembered very clearly because it had bothered me at the time.

She glanced at her notes again and back at me. "The day before Philip was shot."

"My mother says a lot of things, including that one day *I'm* going to kill *her*. You can't take what she says seriously."

"Does your father own a rifle?"

Another zinger. And she got me again.

"Doesn't everyone around here?" I volleyed.

"That doesn't answer my question." She slapped her pen down on the table.

If she thought she was going to intimidate me, she was wrong. However, I couldn't lie to her. "Yes, my father owns several guns. So do a lot of men in this county, some of whom would have loved to see Philip dead."

"Answer my question," she snapped. "Does he own a rifle?"

"Yes," I said.

"What kind?"

"Two." I took a deep breath. "A regular shotgun and a 30-06."

She eyed me with her flat glance. "Don't make things rough for yourself, Mrs. Cunningham. And remember what I told you. Don't interfere with my investigation."

I stood and slung my purse over my shoulder. "I've done nothing to prevent you from doing your job. I gave you something I found. I've answered any question you've asked me. Am I free to go?"

She stood, too. "Yes. You may go."

I walked from the barracks to my car, shaking. I'd always had a deep regard for law enforcement officers, despite what I'd said to Eric about their attitudes, but Detective Reid was pushing my limits.

⁓

Back at home, I was standing in front of the clothes dryer folding socks, wondering if I would like doing laundry any better if I had a large laundry room like Hayley's. With lots of storage and a top-of-the-line washer and dryer. With a family our size, laundry is one chore that is never done in our house. I don't particularly enjoy it, but at the moment, I was glad for the seemingly insurmountable pile of clothes waiting to be sorted then washed, dried, and put away.

I turned my attention to a basket of dirty clothes and began checking pockets. As usual, I found stuff in Sammie's pockets. A screw, a stone, and an empty Tootsie Roll wrapper. I shook Angelica's words from my mind.

This was normal behavior for a kid.

My interview with Detective Reid had left me with a feeling of foreboding that I couldn't shake, like I was waiting for the other shoe to drop. So when my mother called me an hour later in a frenzy, I wasn't surprised.

"Trish, your father just called me. The police have a search warrant, and they're taking his hunting rifles from the barn. I had trouble understanding him on the phone. He said something about Buddy, but he was so upset, I couldn't understand him. I can't be there. I have to go down to the state police barracks for an interview." Her words were breathless, not like her normal harsh tone.

"I was just there myself. Watch out for Detective Reid—"

She interrupted me with a string of words about the detective that were surprisingly uncomplimentary, even from my acerbic mother. Under normal circumstances, I might have been shocked and amused. However, my concern right now was my father. He was such a calm man. That Ma said he was unintelligible on the phone meant he was very upset. Things were bad.

"I should stop by the farm first," my mother said.

"You don't want to keep the detective waiting," I said. "It'll just make her nastier. How about I go over to the farm and see what's going on with Daddy."

"Good." I heard the relief in her voice. "Thank you."

When I arrived at the farm, the last state trooper was pulling from the driveway. I pulled up next to the house and hopped from the car, wondering if Daddy was in the house or the barn. His truck was next to the barn, but that meant nothing. I headed to the house first. Then I heard the squeal of the barn door and turned to see Daddy walking from the barn with Buddy lying limp in his arms. He didn't see me.

"Daddy?" I dropped my purse to the ground and ran to meet him.

He glanced in my direction and stopped.

When I reached him, he had tears on his cheeks. I didn't need to be told. Buddy was dead.

"What happened?"

He swallowed. "The stress was too much, sugar bug. If I'd known they were coming, I would have put him in the house." He laid Buddy in the back of his truck with such gentleness that I began to cry. Then he turned to me. "I'm going to bury him in the field. Will you come with me? Your mother wouldn't be able to do it."

"Yes. You know I will." I threw my arms around his neck, and even while I tried to comfort him, anger filled my gut, so red and hot that I shook. The old Trish, the redneck who never used to think twice about taking on anyone in a fight for right, warred inside me with the new Trish. The good Christian mommy who was trying hard to be a nice person.

At the moment, old Trish was winning. I wished with all my heart that I could grab Detective Reid by the hair and beat her up.

Daddy stepped back and saw my face and shook his head. "I see that flash in your eyes."

"They had no right." I gulped and took a deep breath to control my temper. "They murdered our dog."

"No." Daddy pushed aside the hair hanging over my eyes. "It was his time. I knew when I woke up this morning that he was going to go soon. He didn't eat, just stuck close by me, and you know how he liked his kibble."

"Still. He didn't need to go like this."

"That's what I thought at first, too." Daddy's eyes bored deep into mine. "But I've got to tell you, I'm not so sure about it anymore. For just a couple of minutes after the police got here, Buddy woke up. Like his old self. Got all protective." Daddy's mouth quirked into a trembly smile. "When I told him to back down, he looked at me with that little doggy grin of his."

I smiled at the memory even while I blinked back tears. Throughout his life, when Buddy knew he was out of line, he used to roll back his upper lip, like he was laughing at us.

Daddy turned and shut the tailgate, then glanced at me over his shoulder. "Maybe this was a good way for him to go. With honor." He waved at the pasture. "I'm going to bury him in his favorite place."

I knew exactly where he meant. "I'll go get two shovels while you open the gate."

He nodded.

Shortly, I joined Daddy in the truck. He stared straight ahead, lips pressed firmly together. As the truck bounced down the hill to the creek at the bottom of the pasture, I wondered if Philip's last choices before he died meant that he died an honorable death, too.

When we reached a small peninsula jutting into the water, Daddy stopped and turned off the engine. Then he stared out the windshield with an unfocused gaze.

"Remember how Buddy always came down here when I mowed the field in the summer? How he used to run through the water?"

"Yep, I do." I smiled as I recalled the little black-and-white bundle of irrepressible energy Buddy had been when Daddy brought him home.

Daddy turned to me and returned my smile. "I thought I'd lost him that first day I brought him out here. He was running so hard that he ran straight off those rocks, right into the creek."

"Yeah. And then you couldn't keep him out of the water after that."

Daddy still smiled, but his eyes had filled with tears. Mine did the same.

"Guess we should get it done," he said gruffly.

"Yep."

We buried Buddy on a piece of high ground, next to the rocks overlooking the creek. When we'd finished, Daddy leaned against his shovel. I put my arm around his waist, and we stood quietly together, both of us lost in our own thoughts.

Then Daddy sighed. "I'm worried."

"Why?"

"The deputy in charge asked me if anyone else had used my guns." He turned to face me. "I had to say yes. The last time I used that 30-06 was when I brought Abbie out here in this field to shoot it."

The panic I'd been fighting since Ma found Philip's body returned, gnawing my insides.

"I didn't want to have to tell them, but I had no choice. Her fingerprints will be on it, anyway. I hope she won't think I'm a traitor." A small tic appeared at the corner of his mouth. "She's like a daughter to me, you know."

His expression was so pained, I rushed to assure him. "She won't think that. She knows you have to tell the truth. She had to tell the truth, as well."

"I just hope it doesn't make things worse," Daddy said.

"Me, too." But even as I tried to sound assuring, I knew things *had* just gotten worse for Abbie. And I needed to work harder to solve this mystery before she ended up in jail.

I bounced against Max as the hay wagon bringing us back from the corn maze jostled to a stop in front of a big red barn. The owners had placed thermal containers of hot chocolate and Styrofoam cups on tables for guests, along with supplies for s'mores. Chris babbled in my arms, pointing with a chubby finger at two roaring bonfires where visitors could roast marshmallows. For once, he wasn't grumpy.

Charlie and Sammie leaped off the wagon and headed for the hot chocolate.

Max kissed me. "You haven't said a word about Abbie or the investigation."

We'd left the house immediately after he'd gotten home from work. The only thing I'd had time to tell him about was Buddy.

"I'm trying to be normal for a few hours." I smiled at him.

He hopped off the wagon and turned to take Chris from me. I slipped to the ground and swiped hay from my jeans.

We followed slowly behind Charlie and Sammie. She was giggling at something he'd whispered in her ear. Chris grinned at me from Max's shoulder. He always seemed happier when we were all together. Was it possible that my dissatisfaction with life was affecting my children? Could that be the reason for Sammie's insecurities and Chris's fussiness?

I reached for Max's spare hand, but before I could grasp it, I heard a familiar voice behind me. I whirled around in time to see Jaylene Adler holding the hand of a young girl, walking toward the pasture where guests were parking their cars.

Jaylene must have sensed my stare. She glanced over her shoulder, saw me, and glared. Then she pulled the girl in front of her, as though shielding her, and kept walking.

"Max." I yanked at his arm. "I have to talk to Jaylene."

"Honey—"

"I'm sorry." I ran after her. "Jaylene! Please wait. I want to talk to you."

She picked up her pace, and the girl had trouble keeping up. I called to her again. When she reached her car, she whirled around and heaved a sigh. "What?"

"I just want to talk to you for a minute."

"Fine." She unlocked the car then leaned down and whispered something in the child's ear. She obediently got inside.

Suddenly Jaylene turned on me so quickly that I thought she was going to hit me.

I felt a hand on my shoulder and realized that Max

had followed me. I leaned back against him, grateful for his presence.

Jaylene looked from me to him. Chris babbled, and from the corner of my eye, I saw him reach an arm out to her. Her mouth twisted into a grimace.

She met my gaze. "We've known you all of our lives, but that doesn't give you the right to pry."

Max tightened his grip on my shoulder.

"All I'm interested in is keeping my best friend out of jail," I said. "And finding the truth about who killed Philip. If you didn't do it, why should you worry?"

"I know you're trying to pin it on Henry," she said. "He might be a louse sometimes with a bad temper, but he's not a killer."

I shook my head. "You don't understand. Like you said, I've known you all my life. I care for you and Henry. I'm not out to pin it on him."

She tapped her foot. "Then why don't you leave us alone?"

"Because I think you have some answers I need."

She crossed her arms. "There's nothing I know that will help you. Nothing."

I took a deep breath. "I found a piece of a letter from Philip that I believe came from your store."

Jaylene's eyes widened. I felt Max stiffen behind me. I felt bad. I hadn't had the time to tell him about it.

"What are you going to do with it?" Jaylene whispered.

"I had no choice," I said. "I've already given it to the police."

Anger suffused her face with red. Her lips trembled.

"I might have known. Just remember this. I won't let you or anyone else hurt my family."

With those words, she whirled around and got into her car. I didn't try to stop her.

Max and I watched her pull from the parking lot.

I felt like a horrible traitor to a family friend.

14

On Saturday morning, I prepared to go talk to Linda and then take Sammie to see her kitten. Max took the rest of the kids out for their regular weekend outing with him. He left me with a stern "Be careful today, and call me to let me know exactly where you are." I didn't blame him. I was disturbed, too. But for more reason than that. I was making no headway with the mystery.

As I pulled my keys from my now neat purse, I noticed something gold sparkling on the bottom. The smashed gold button. There was a clue I hadn't pursued yet, and today was the perfect opportunity.

An hour later, I stood in Hayley's kitchen with her and Angelica, fingering the button in my pants pocket. Sammie was playing with the kittens in the laundry room. Hayley's face looked drawn and tense.

When something soft brushed my leg, I jumped. Then I looked down. Mr. Chang Lee was perched next to my right foot. He met my gaze and yowled. I crossed my arms, looked away, and hoped for the best. I still didn't trust him.

Angelica's eyes widened as she stared down at him. "I've never seen him accept anyone else but Hayley."

I relaxed a fraction. That was good news from an objective source.

"From the first time Trish showed up, he acted that way," Hayley said.

Angelica shook her head. "That's amazing."

"I'm so glad you both came over," Hayley said, but she was focused on Angelica. I was surprised they didn't make little kissy sounds at each other.

"Would you like iced tea?" Hayley turned to me. "Coffee? Lemonade?"

"Do you have Mountain Dew?" I asked.

"I don't have that, but I have other sodas," Hayley said.

"It's fine. I'll take coffee." The time was drawing near to break my addiction.

"I'll take the same." Angelica took some mugs out of the cupboard.

Angelica had no idea where the coffee mugs were in my cupboards.

"So, Trish," Hayley said after she ground coffee beans and began preparing the coffee in a professional-style, stainless steel coffeemaker. "Angelica tells me you like to solve mysteries. You've been involved in two, and you're looking into the death of this Philip fellow?"

I glanced at my mother-in-law, surprised she'd said anything. "I do it only when I need to—to protect someone. At first I thought it was intriguing, like solving a puzzle, but then I started counting the cost for my family. It can be dangerous."

"I told Leighton what you were doing. He said he'd never allow me to do anything like that. He says it could be too dangerous." Hayley shuddered and rubbed her arms.

I felt a stab of resentment at her insinuation that Max didn't care enough for me, and I wanted to say, *At least my husband isn't seeing another woman.* Not that I knew for certain that Leighton *was* seeing Linda.

"Murder is so terrible," Hayley said. "And so awful for

your friend. He was her husband, right?"

I shook my head. "Ex."

I wasn't real happy that Leighton Whitmore knew about my sleuthing. He was still a suspect in my book, no matter what. For that matter, so was Hayley.

Well, now was as good a time as any to pursue my latest line of questioning. I pulled the button from my pocket.

"Is this yours?" I asked Hayley.

She leaned over to stare at it. "No. I don't recognize it. Why?"

"I just found it and wondered."

My question hadn't made an impression on Hayley at all, but Angelica was studying me with narrowed eyes. She knew what I was doing.

The coffeemaker burbled on the counter, and the smell of coffee began to permeate the air.

"It's just hard to believe something like that could happen around here," Hayley said.

"Too unpleasant to think about," Angelica added.

I took that as a cue to change the subject. What I needed to know could be learned without talking about Philip. "So is Leighton retired?" I asked.

"Not exactly. He was supposed to be, but. . .anyway, he's happier working." Hayley didn't look at me; she just watched the coffee drip into the pot.

"What did he do when he worked full-time?"

She crossed her arms. "Real estate. . .construction. A long time ago he had a law degree." She finally looked at me. "What do you take in your coffee?"

"Just cream." Her answer was rather unrevealing. I'd

try a blunt question. "Do you know Linda King?"

Hayley's gaze slid to the wall. "Linda King?"

"She's a real estate agent. She works part-time for my mother. I just thought you might know her. She acted like she knew you. Talked about your cats."

"Oh, *that* Linda King. Yes." Hayley swallowed and straightened her shoulders. "I know *of* her."

Angelica met my gaze over Hayley's shoulder and shook her head slightly.

Hayley sniffed, and I realized she was almost in tears.

Was Leighton having an affair with Linda? Did Hayley suspect?

"I'm sorry," I said, although I wasn't sure what I was apologizing about.

"No, it's not you," she said.

Angelica put a hand on Hayley's shoulder. "Why don't you go sit down? I'll get the coffee."

Hayley nodded and went to the family room.

"They might be moving," Angelica whispered as she walked by me to the counter. "That woman is their real estate agent. Hayley doesn't want to leave, and she's upset."

So Leighton's meeting with Linda could be totally innocent. She was going to sell their house.

Angelica handed me my cup of coffee and then carried hers and Hayley's to the family room. They sat on the couch. I settled in a comfy chair facing the french doors that led to the pool. Why were Leighton and Hayley moving now? After all the trouble and expense of the pool?

Mr. Chang Lee jumped up in my chair and settled

next to me, his body resting against my thigh. For once, I welcomed his attention. He was communicating happiness with his purrs—at least I assumed it was happiness. That was better than the stilted attempts at conversation between me, Angelica, and Hayley. I felt like the proverbial third wheel and wondered if I was the cause of the awkwardness. Perhaps Hayley wanted to talk about her troubles, and I was preventing her from doing so.

I had already decided to leave when Sammie came running into the room.

Angelica's face lit up.

"When can I take my kitten home?" Sammie asked Hayley.

"Tuesday," Hayley said.

Sammie clapped her hands. Angelica continued to gaze at her with bright eyes. I'd never watched her face around the children before. I felt my heart constrict. My bad attitude had prevented me from seeing anything good about my mother-in-law.

Hayley smiled. "Angelica has a class Wednesday night."

"A class?" I asked.

"She's taking a citizen police academy class," Hayley said.

"What did you say?" I was positive I hadn't heard Hayley correctly. I glanced at Angelica, and she was blushing.

Hayley smiled. "I told Angelica it would be the perfect way for her to understand more about what Tommy's going to do." Her smile faded. "We were both going to do it, but Leighton said it wasn't a good idea for me right now."

"It's fine. I can do it alone." Angelica patted Hayley's

arm then turned to me. "If Tommy insists upon pursuing law enforcement, I've decided to support him. Max assured me that it was Tommy's choice and not something"—she glanced at me—"not something he was talked into."

I understood what she was saying. She thought I was just as controlling as I thought *she* was. This was her way of explaining. Maybe even trying to apologize. To say I was amazed at what she was doing would be an understatement.

I did the only thing I could.

"Angelica, the kitten is a gift from you. It would be special if you're here with us when Sammie picks up her cat. Then maybe you and Andrew can come to our house for dinner that night to celebrate." I glanced down at my lap then back up at her. "And if you do want company at that class, I'll go with you."

Angelica's surprised smile told me everything I needed to know.

—————

Linda's office was in downtown Four Oaks, just one block down from Abbie's apartment. The windows of the real estate business were plastered with pictures of houses for sale.

"Don't pick anything up," I whispered to Sammie as we walked through the door.

"Mommy. . ."

Inside, I smelled coffee and some kind of cinnamon air freshener. Several agents sat at their desks. Linda was perched on the edge of hers, chatting on the phone. She saw me, smiled, and held up one finger.

I settled Sammie on a chair with a book to read. I didn't have to wait long. When Linda was done talking, she slid off her desk and reached into a bowl on her desk. Then she walked over to us and handed Sammie a Tootsie Roll. Sammie grinned, unwrapped the candy, and stuffed it in her mouth.

"Come and tell me what you're looking for."

I explained our criteria. "I don't want to look today. I'd just like some listings to show Max."

She rested her elbows on the desk. "So what area are you interested in?"

I needed to find a way to bring up the Whitmores. "Do you have anything out Brownsville way?"

Her eyes lit up. The houses out there were expensive. "Yes, I do."

"My in-laws live out there," I said. "And we're also getting a Siamese kitten from Hayley Whitmore."

"Yes, your mother told me that." Her brown eyes reminded me of the button eyes on Sammie's stuffed bear. No expression at all. "So how many bedrooms do you want?"

I told her and wondered if my trip here was going to be wasted.

She turned her gaze to her computer screen and tap-tapped on her keyboard. As she sifted through listings on her computer, sending some to a printer across the room, I studied her desk. Lots of pink stuff, including several pink ceramic picture frames. Most of the pictures featured Linda. Two were taken in the same place, in front of a fountain. It looked familiar to me, but I couldn't place it.

I pointed at it. "Is this a vacation you took? Looks like fun."

She nodded. "Yes, I went to a real estate convention last year in Atlanta. I stayed an extra week with some friends and toured everything. I met some interesting people there." The printer hummed in the background. She continued to chat about everything and nothing.

I decided to interrupt her. "I met Clark Matthews's mother the other day. Eunice?"

"Oh?" Linda asked.

"I took her an autographed bookplate from Abbie. She thinks very highly of you."

"She's a nice lady," Linda said.

"She's happy that Clark is living with her and doing so well. Like taking classes at the junior college and volunteering at the YMCA. She says he's not happy at his job, though."

Linda shot me a gaze. "Sometimes she exaggerates." Then she stood. "I think that's about all the listings I can find right now."

I was desperate. I stood, too, and yanked the button from my pocket. "Is this yours?"

For a moment, her eyes narrowed. She took the button from my hand then dropped it back into my palm. "I don't think so, but even if it was, it's too damaged to do me any good." She stepped around her chair. "Now I'll go get the listings."

While she was doing that, I stared at the pictures. I suddenly remembered where I had seen a similar fountain. In the picture on Hayley's mantel. But Hayley had said it was her wedding photograph. I had assumed they'd gotten married in New York City. Did they get married in Atlanta? And was this even significant?

When Linda returned with the papers, she covered the main points about each property. I pretended to pay attention, but I didn't hear a word she said. I had one more doubt in my head about Leighton and Hayley Whitmore. And I knew in my heart that time was running out for Abbie.

15

I was so discouraged on Sunday that all I wanted to do was go back to bed after church. Knowing that Philip was being buried added to my blues. Abbie felt similarly. I'd talked to her earlier when we confirmed that she and Eric were joining me, Max, and the kids at my mother's for Sunday supper.

At the moment, Karen was on the phone in her room. Charlie and Sammie were in the family room watching an old Sherlock Holmes movie on television. Max was in the living room with his nose buried in the newspaper, and I'd just put Chris down for a nap.

Only one thing would help my mental state. Solving Philip's murder. I grabbed my notebook from my purse and joined Max. I needed to write down the clue about the picture on the Whitmores' mantel.

He saw what I had in my hands, sighed, and put the paper on the coffee table. I thought he might be about to lecture me about my sleuthing and opened my mouth to protest.

"Maybe I can help," he said. "I know you're discouraged. You want to talk it all through with me?"

"Really?" I grinned.

"Really," he said.

"Do you realize this is the first time you've offered to help me with an investigation?"

"I guess it is. What is it that your mother says? If you can't beat 'em, join 'em?"

"Yep, among a million other clichés."

He stood and pointed at the couch. "Let's sit."

I snuggled next to him. "So why are you helping me?"

"I want this solved. I want it over."

I shared his sentiments. Despite the comfort of his solid body next to mine, I felt uneasy. Like a storm cloud was rushing toward me and I needed to find shelter.

He tapped my notebook. "Well, tell me what you have so far. Maybe I'll see a connection you've missed."

One by one, we went through the clues. When we were done, I looked up at him. His eyes were narrowed.

"I have to agree with you. Philip was so determined to make things right with everyone he'd wronged, that seems the most likely reason he was killed. Jaylene was awfully hostile on Friday night." His brows were drawn into a deep V. Jaylene's hostility had frightened both of us.

"That leads me to my suspects." I flipped to another page. "What do you think?"

Max read down the list then pointed at Leighton's name. "Why are Leighton and Hayley on here?"

I felt defensive. "I know they're your family's friends, but I have my reasons. More him than her, though."

"Go on." Max's face was unusually blank.

"Well, like all the others, I know he was at the fall festival. Hayley told me. And Philip saw something there that made him leave in a hurry."

"Anything else?" Max asked.

"Well, he's from New York. And. . ." I hesitated.

"And?"

I told Max about the picture on the mantel.

"Are you sure you're remembering right?" he asked.

"I'm sure," I said. "And then I saw him at a restaurant with Linda King. Now he and Hayley might be moving. Something just isn't right. I'm not sure what."

Max blinked. "They're moving?"

"I found out yesterday when Sammie was visiting her kitten."

"I hadn't heard that yet," Max said. "I'll be honest with you, though. Despite the way my mother champions Leighton, I've never felt right about him."

"What about your father?" I asked.

"He agrees with me." Max grimaced. "I think my mother felt sorry for Hayley and just wanted her to be happy."

The doorbell rang. "I'll get it!" Charlie yelled, sliding down the hall to the front door.

"Can you explain what you mean about Leighton?" I asked Max.

"Not really," he said.

"Mom! It's for you," Charlie yelled. "It's a lady."

"Go on," Max said. "There's nothing else I can tell you. Really."

Charlie was regaling our visitor with chatter about the movie he was watching. I walked from the living room and felt the cold November breeze sweep down the hall, the perfect prelude for the entrance of the woman with the grief-lined face who stood on my front porch. Mary Grenville, Philip's sister. She wore a black wool coat over a simple black dress that emphasized her pale skin, red-rimmed eyes, and drawn face that looked like a wax mask.

"Thank you, Charlie," I said. He scampered away to

continue watching his movie.

"Come in." I opened the door wide.

She brushed past me then stood in the foyer with her arms crossed. "My mother said you wanted to talk to me, so I stopped by. I hope it's okay."

"It's fine. I have a few hours before I have to get ready to go out."

I took her coat and draped it over the coatrack.

Max walked into the hallway, and I introduced them.

"I'm so sorry about your brother," he said.

"Thank you."

Max turned to me. "Why don't you two go into the living room? I'll make sure the kids leave you alone."

"Thank you," I whispered as we walked past him.

He squeezed my hand then walked away.

Mary and I settled on the couch in the living room, then tears began to fall down her cheeks. She swiped at them with the back of her hands. "I'm sorry. I made it through the burial without crying."

"I'm so sorry," I said. "I can't even imagine how hard this has been for you."

"It's not like this was unexpected. His death, I mean. I just didn't expect the emotions to hit me so hard." She took a deep breath then pulled herself together, gathering her emotions and covering them with a shell of self-control, almost like putting on a coat.

Her lips were now set in a firm line. Her eyes weren't hostile, but her gaze was steady. "You've been asking my mother questions about Philip."

"Yes." I wondered if she was going to ream me out for being a pest.

"She says you're trying to solve his murder?" She eyed me with wariness. "You're not just curious about him, are you? Or trying to make him look bad? Because of Abbie?"

I liked the fact that she was blunt. It would make our conversation easier. "Yes, I'm trying to solve his murder. To clear Abbie, not to make him look bad. But if he ends up looking bad because of what my investigation reveals, that's out of my control. I'm sorry."

She met my gaze with her unblinking one. "That's honest, and I appreciate it. There are some things you should know. I'd rather tell you than that detective. She left my mother in tears." Mary's nostrils flared. "There is no excuse for leaving a grieving mother in that state."

"The detective isn't on anyone's most popular list right now," I said.

Her hands clenched into fists in her lap. "That's an understatement. I'm going to make sure I'm there the next time Reid talks to my mother."

I wished I could be there for that.

"I'm going to start back over a year ago," she said. "I think what I say will help you."

"Do you mind if I take notes?" I hesitated to without her permission.

She waved her hand. "Fine with me."

I pulled my notebook from the coffee table where Max had put it. When I was settled, she began.

"When Philip got sick, I went and stayed with him while he went through chemo. We hadn't been close since we were kids, but he begged me to come." She pulled at the fabric of her dress. "I'm ashamed to say it now, but I didn't want to do it. He'd been such an awful person, and I hated being around him, even if he was my brother."

"I can understand that," I murmured.

"I finally did after Mom begged me to. She couldn't because she had to work." She paused. "Mom told you about his conversion, right?"

I nodded.

A tiny smile played on her lips. "I don't share my mother's strong faith, but I recognize true change when I see it. I knew he was different as soon as I walked through the door to his apartment. He hugged me."

"That must have made you happy."

"Yes, but I didn't understand at first. Only that he was somehow different. Unfortunately, that wasn't the only change." The light in her eyes died. "His face was haggard. He looked like a scarecrow that had lost its stuffing. It's funny, but when someone is dying of an illness like cancer, it seems to permeate everything. At least that's the way it seemed with him." She paused. "It was odd, but even before chemo, he seemed to know he was going to die. Going for treatment was just going through the motions."

"I can't imagine what that was like for you," I said again.

She acknowledged my comment with a nod. "Not unless you've watched a friend or relative go through it. And to make it worse, I'd just lost a lot of money in a real estate scam, so I was feeling really low anyway."

She glanced at me. "Now things weren't perfect. Philip had changed, but he still had secrets."

"What kinds of secrets?" I asked.

She shrugged. "Probably a lot more than I will ever

know. But I wanted to know what really happened with Abbie. He refused to talk about it. Said he needed to make that right with her before he'd say anything to anyone." Mary picked at a fingernail. "I like Abbie. We were never close, but I felt like she got a bad deal when she married my brother. The old Philip was a brutal man."

"Yes," I said.

She clasped her hands together. "I don't want Abbie accused of this murder. I know for certain it wasn't her. I'm convinced this had something to do with Philip's past. Or something that he knew about someone."

"That's what I think, too," I said. "Why do you say that?"

"Because he returned home to make amends and probably talked to someone who didn't want to make things right."

"Do you have any thoughts about that? Any ideas?"

"Two." She shifted on the couch and dropped her gaze to the carpet. "This is hard to say. I feel like I'm giving away his secrets, even though he's dead." She looked up at me. "I didn't tell the police about this. I just couldn't. Because it doesn't just affect Philip." After a deep breath, she met my gaze. "You must promise me that no one will know unless it's necessary."

"But if it's necessary to keep Abbie from prison, I can tell?"

After the briefest hesitation, she nodded. "I know that sooner or later it will come out. I just need a couple of days to tell my mother. I don't want her hurt any more than she already is right now."

"All right. You have my word. But why are you trusting

me with something so important to you?"

"For Abbie. Because it was so important to Philip that he make amends with her. I don't want to see her accused of something she didn't do." Mary took a deep breath. "Philip had a weak moment during his hospital stay. He saw a little girl pass by his door, and he started to cry. I asked him why. He said it was because he had a daughter, but he wasn't allowed to see her."

I felt the shock of her words physically. "A daughter? Where?"

"Here," Mary said. "Seems that was part of the reason he left town. He and Abbie weren't doing well. And he was being threatened by the father of the girl he got pregnant." Mary's lips twisted into a grimace. "I suspect she was underage."

"That could have ruined his career." I stated the obvious.

"Yeah. Whoever it was had mercy on him, I guess. Or maybe they just didn't want their daughter involved in a scandal like that." Mary bit one of her nails. "After that day in the hospital, he never said another word about it. I asked him about it again—once—and he told me to forget it. But I think he wanted to see his daughter. To meet her before he died."

Something of that magnitude certainly could lead to hostility. My mind immediately flitted to Jaylene's daughter, Peggy. I had a vague memory of her leaving town and returning later on, married and with a baby. The child we saw her with at the corn maze looked to be the right age.

I looked at Mary. "I assume Abbie doesn't know this. She never said anything. I think she should know.

It would be horrible if it came out in the investigation." Even coming from me, the news could push an already emotionally battered Abbie over the edge.

Mary frowned, and I hastened to make my case. "Think about how humiliating it would be for her to find out from Detective Reid."

Mary's eyes flashed at the mention of Detective Reid's name. "That woman! Okay. I agree with you. In fact, I could see Detective Reid uncovering that and using it to try to make Abbie confess something." She paused for just a heartbeat. "And if you have to, tell Eric. It might help the investigation. I'll tell my mother as soon as possible." Mary smiled sadly. "With Philip dead, it's just me, and I'm not particularly the marrying kind. I know Mom would love to know she had a grandchild, but what if the woman's family doesn't want my mother involved at all? The possible complications are too much to think about right now."

I agreed, and I didn't want June hurt more, either. Still, she had a core of strength I wasn't sure Mary saw. Perhaps living with her mother would help Mary see that.

"You said you had two ideas. Do you know anything else that might help?" I asked. "Do you think there's a possibility that his murder had anything to do with work? Like a case he was investigating?"

Mary shook her head. "I can't answer that. The last job he'd had was in narcotics, but he'd been out of work for almost six months. Would it take that long for something to catch up with him?"

Probably not. "Is there anything else you can think of that was bothering him?"

"Yeah." She grimaced. "Me. Well, I mean, what had

happened to me. I lost money in a real estate scam. It was quite the scandal. I couldn't believe I'd been sucked in. Two men were jailed, but the ones at the top got away scot-free. Philip wanted to fix that for me before he died. Get my money back."

My mind veered right to Leighton Whitmore. He was into real estate. He had been in Atlanta—presumably to get married. But he was from New York.

I met Mary's gaze. "Those are two really powerful motivations for murder."

~

After Mary left, I immediately called Nick Fletcher and told him everything she'd told me about Philip's daughter and added my suspicions about the Adlers. Finally, I reiterated my misgivings about Leighton Whitmore. I told him about the real estate scam in Atlanta. He didn't say much, but I could tell he was listening.

"And worst of all," I said, "I don't know what to do about Abbie. This daughter of Philip's could push her over the edge."

"Tell Eric, Mrs. C.," he said. "Let him tell her."

The idea was perfect. And Corporal Fletcher sounded more upbeat than he had the last few times we'd talked, so when we finally hung up, I felt encouraged.

After that, Max and I got the kids ready and we headed to my folks' house. Karen had gone to visit a friend, so we just had the three youngest. We hadn't found the time to discuss my visit with Mary.

"You're quiet," Max said as we drove.

I didn't want to say much in front of Charlie and Sammie. I motioned with my eyes toward the backseat.

He nodded and reached for my hand.

I took his and squeezed. "Max, I've been thinking recently about how selfish I am. I think if I were facing the end of my life, I wouldn't want to frantically try to make things right with people."

"Oh?" Max asked.

"I have a couple of things I need to do now. And I need to start with your mother."

His surprise was obvious by his upraised brows. "My mother?"

"Yes." I glanced at the backseat. "I'll tell you more later. Just know that things are going to change for the better. At least on my side."

"Really?" The tiny smile on his face cut me to the core. I suddenly realized how hard my hostility had been on him, despite his humor and understanding.

"I'm so sorry," I whispered.

When we got to the farm, I asked him to wait after the kids hopped from the car. Max reached to get Chris from his car seat, and briefly I told him what Mary had said.

"Whew!" he said. "Things just seem to keep getting worse. Are you going to tell Abbie?"

I fingered my coat zipper. "I'm going to let Eric do it. But first, I need to talk to Ma about the Adlers without telling her why I'm asking."

Getting my mother to talk about Jaylene and Henry wasn't hard. Ma was angry that Jaylene wasn't speaking to her. Ma confirmed that Jaylene's daughter, Peggy, had a child out of wedlock. Nine years ago. No one ever knew who the father was. Everyone assumed it was one of two boys she was dating at the time. Jaylene and Henry had sent Peggy to a private school that allowed her to raise her daughter and graduate at the same time. Despite the fact that unwed mothers were relatively common at the time, Jaylene and Henry wanted to avoid the stigma Peggy would have lived under in Four Oaks.

We sat down to eat shortly after Abbie and Eric arrived. Dinner was subdued, despite the chattering of the children and Chris's constant babbling. Ma kept offering everyone food. Max and Eric tried valiantly to keep the conversation flowing. I made an effort to eat, even though I felt sick to my stomach holding the secrets Mary had spilled to me.

Charlie kept eyeing Eric. Finally, he put his fork down. "Uncle Eric, Mike says his brother might have to go to juvie jail."

Eric met Charlie's gaze. "Really?"

Sammie squirmed in her chair.

"Yup. Drugs." Charlie looked at me. "What was it called?"

"Ecstasy," I said, staring at the Mountain Dew in my glass.

"Big problem right now," Eric said. "Especially with the under-twenty-five crowd."

"I read about that in the paper," Max said. "How they hide tablets in candy and—"

"Aunt Abbie, are you going to jail?" Sammie blurted out.

Ma gasped. Abbie blanched.

"No, she's not," I snapped. "We told you that already."

"But—"

Eric smiled, but it was strained. "We aren't going to let your aunt Abbie go to jail, honey. People go to jail when they do very bad things. Aunt Abbie didn't do anything bad."

"Mom won't let her go to jail, either," Charlie said. "She's investigating. Things will be fine."

"Mommy is good at that," Sammie said.

My children were my biggest supporters. Unlike Eric Scott. I picked at my nails to avoid his eyes.

"Well, I should say so." Ma waved her fork to emphasize her words. "I don't want to be critical of the police, Eric, but I don't understand how that Detective Reid person can begin to solve the crime if she's focused on only one person. We all know it wasn't Abbie. Right, Simon?"

"Yes, we know Abbie isn't guilty," Daddy said. "But we don't know for sure who the police are looking at."

"Well," Ma huffed. "They're looking at Abbie."

This conversation wasn't making things better. I glanced at my friend, who was studiously avoiding everyone's eyes.

Daddy had been quiet most of the meal. He kept glancing surreptitiously at Abbie, and I knew he felt guilty about the gun, even though it wasn't his fault.

My mother launched into a discussion about Daddy's search for a new dog. A friend of a friend had a litter of border collies. Then Sammie began jabbering about her new kitten.

With the change of topic, Abbie relaxed. When dinner was about over, she took Eric's hand and looked at my father.

"Simon," she said.

He blinked and looked at her.

"I. . .we. . .have something to ask you."

Daddy clenched his jaw.

"If things work out—"

"*When* things work out," Eric corrected.

Abbie swallowed. "*When* things work out, we want to know if you'll walk me down the aisle. Since I don't have a father to ask and you've been like a dad to me."

Daddy's mouth opened and shut like a goldfish. Then a big tear rolled down his cheek.

"Yes," he said.

Ma's grin couldn't have been bigger.

After dinner, Abbie was helping Ma clear the table. I pulled Eric into the hallway near the stairs under the pretense of a secret wedding surprise for Abbie.

"What is it?" he asked.

"I talked to Philip's sister today," I said. "I have something to tell you. Well, Corporal Fletcher suggested I tell you. He said you'd be the best one to tell Abbie."

Eric's expression was like that of a man who had been hit too many times. "Okay. Go on."

I told him in as few words as possible about Philip's confession and his child.

"Oh man." He rubbed his face with his hand. "Can things get worse?"

"Yes, they can," I said. "Abbie can go to jail."

I glanced at the door to the kitchen through which we

could hear the low murmurs of Ma's and Abbie's voices. "I'm worried that Detective Reid will find out and try to use it somehow against her. And I think Henry and Jaylene Adler's grandchild is Philip's daughter."

He reached out and tapped his finger on the banister. Then he looked at me. "I can't speculate with you."

"I know." I had to be satisfied with that answer.

16

I woke to the phone ringing. I snatched it from the bedside table and held it to my ear. But I didn't need to in order to hear my mother. She was yelling.

"Jaylene just called me. Said Henry was taken in by the state police for hours yesterday evening, thanks to you."

"At least they're looking at someone else and not just Abbie," I said.

"Well, she's threatening to sue you and us," Ma said.

Great. Just what I needed. Something else to worry about.

"She said we would pay one way or another."

Apprehension wiggled on the back of my neck. "Did she say it like that?" I asked.

Ma hesitated. "Well, not exactly, but that was the gist of it."

"All right. I've gotta go. The kids will be getting up soon."

I hung up then turned to Max, who was lying next to me with his arms behind his head. "Your mother," he stated. "I heard her voice through the receiver."

"Hard to miss." I lay on my side, head cradled in my hand.

"So what's up?"

I relayed the context of the conversation.

His face tightened. "Maybe I should talk to one of my friends, have someone go by the Adlers' store. These threats are going to stop right now."

I stared at Max in admiration. As long as I didn't have to personally deal with his lawyer friends and he wasn't getting bossy with *me*, I loved it when he took control.

He rolled on his side and ran his hand down my arm. "I have some good news for you. I think it will make you happy." He touched the end of my nose. "I was going to wait until Abbie's situation cleared up, but this might be a good distraction for you."

"I'm not sure I need a distraction," I said. "I need to solve this murder."

"Yes, but maybe giving it a rest will allow your brain a chance to regroup, so to speak, maybe see things in a different way."

"What is it?"

"A job," he said.

I jerked my gaze to meet his. "A job? At Cunningham and Son?"

"Yes and no." He grinned. "We're about to put up the trailer at the construction site for the new housing development. Someone needs to run the office."

I sat up and felt a quiver of excitement in my stomach. "That's perfect. It uses all my skills."

He leaned back against the headboard. "Yes, I know. And, honey, I want you to know you have my blessing whether you decide to go full-time or part-time. Hire someone else to help you if you need to."

"It sounds wonderful," I murmured, and tears started to burn in my eyes.

"You can go out there today, if you'd like. Start to figure out what you need in terms of equipment and things." He frowned. "Baby?"

I buried my head in his shoulder and the tears flowed.

"Hey," he said, stroking my back. "Aren't you happy?"

"Yes," I mumbled into his shoulder. "You're so sweet. And I'm so blessed. But then I think about Abbie and everything, and I feel bad for being happy about anything."

He wrapped his arms around me and pulled me tight to his warm, muscular chest. "I understand."

A bit later, I was pulling on my slippers and Max was walking to the bathroom to take a shower.

"I'm going to the construction site today. I think you're right. A break will help." Despite everything I'd learned, I was beginning to think I would never solve this crime. I just hoped everything I'd told Corporal Fletcher would aid the investigation.

"I think that's good," Max said.

I grabbed my bathrobe from a chair. "Honey, you don't think Leighton Whitmore killed Philip?"

"I don't see how. Since they're moving, I haven't done any more checking into his background. If I were a betting guy, my money would be on Henry Adler."

Mine, too. And that was my biggest problem. I didn't want it to be Henry.

17

I woke on Tuesday feeling guilty that I'd spent all the previous day at the construction job site trailer, figuring out how I was going to set up my new office. I spent the morning going over my clues between catching up on bookkeeping for Max and pacing my kitchen. The break hadn't helped my investigation at all. I was no closer to figuring out who killed Philip than I had been two days previous. I was panicked that Abbie would end up in jail.

With my mind still turning, I dropped Chris off at Gladys's; then Sammie and I were headed to the Whitmores' to pick up her kitten.

I'd asked Max if he thought we'd be safe going there, and he'd said yes. Then Angelica had called me at the last minute to say we needed to get there thirty minutes earlier than planned. Leighton had come home early and wanted to take Hayley out to dinner.

That meant Sammie hadn't had a snack. She was complaining that she was hungry, so I decided to make a pit stop at the Gas 'n' Go. I was once again in an inner struggle, salivating for a Mountain Dew. I vowed to break my habit—but not today. Inside the store, I overheard three teens in line ahead of me order hot dogs. That sounded so good that I ordered hot dogs for me and Sammie.

While we waited for Pat, the clerk, to fix them, I got my Mountain Dew and some juice for Sammie, then we went to the rack of chips. I waited for her to pick out the one she wanted. Through the front window of the store,

I saw Clark pull his blue WWPS truck into a space next to my SUV.

Sammie tugged on my arm. "Mommy, I want these."

I glanced down at the bag of Doritos she held. "Okay, that's fine." I grabbed one for myself. Then it occurred to me that I was giving in to the power of suggestion an awful lot lately. First Mountain Dew, then hot dogs, and now chips.

Our food was ready by the time we got back to the counter. The teens had already paid for theirs and were headed out the door. A rack holding the latest weekly edition of our local paper was next to the counter. The headline was Philip's death. It was now officially a murder investigation, surprise, surprise. Abbie's picture was featured in the article, next to a picture of Philip. I felt sick and glanced away to calm myself. Clark was on the sidewalk, holding a box and talking to the kids.

"He's really built, isn't he?" Pat said as she rang up my order.

I swiveled my head to look at her. "What?"

"That WWPS delivery guy." She grinned like a wolf. "This is my daily eye candy break. He comes in every day at this time to get a drink and a snack."

"Oh." That was one way to put it. But I couldn't have cared less about Clark. Like a magnet, my attention was drawn back to the article. I finally picked up the paper and put it on the counter. "Add this, please."

Pat shook her head. "Isn't that tragic? Seems they're about to arrest that guy's ex-wife. And her being an author and all."

Whatever being an author had to do with anything.

Pat leaned toward me and pointed at Philip's picture in the paper. "You know this Philip guy? He was in here. With her." Pat jabbed at Abbie's picture. "Cops asked me about that. Fact, he and Eye Candy talked once, too."

Clark and Philip had talked? As she continued to chat, I paid for my purchases, took the bag, and handed the paper to Sammie to carry. Then I headed for the car.

The teens had left, and Clark was standing next to his truck. He seemed to be waiting for us. "I wanted to thank you for taking that autograph to my mother."

"She's very proud of you," I said. "Told me you were taking classes and helping kids at the Y."

"Charlie goes to the Y," Sammie said. "His friend's brother was arrested."

Clark glanced down at her then looked up at me.

"Sammie, honey, I don't think Mr. Clark cares about all of that." I smiled at him.

"Charlie is your son, right? I've heard your mother talking about him."

"Yes," I said. I wished my mother would zip her big mouth.

"And I'm getting a kitten today," Sammie informed him. "My grandma bought it for me. It's Siamese and lives in a big house right now."

Clark raised an eyebrow.

I glanced at my watch. "And we're going to be late if we don't get moving."

He smiled at me then told us both good-bye and went into the Gas 'n' Go. A cold breeze whipped my hair in my eyes, and for a moment, I couldn't see. I shoved it aside and dug in my purse for my keys.

As I unlocked the SUV, Sammie dropped the paper on the ground. It fell apart. Perhaps it was just as well. Reading it would just upset me.

"I'm sorry, Mommy." Sammie bent over to pick it up.

"It's okay." I put her food in the back where she could reach it.

The paper was a mess. She handed it to me section by section, and I stuffed it on the floor. After I buckled her into her seat, I shut the door and glanced into the store as I walked around to the driver's side door. Clark was standing at the counter, staring out the window at us. For some reason, he made me uneasy. I decided to review my clues when I got home. If Clark had had contact with Philip, maybe he was the killer. Once again, he moved to the top of my list. I just needed to figure out why.

~

Although Sammie had claimed hunger, she hardly touched her hot dog. When we arrived at the Whitmores', she undid her belt and exploded from the SUV. I followed behind her as quickly as possible. She pressed the doorbell and looked up at me with sparkling eyes.

"The kitty can sleep with me, right?"

"Sure," I said. I hadn't even thought about where the cat would sleep.

Leighton answered the door. "Hello, Trish. We were expecting you. Angelica is already here."

"Can I go on back, Mommy?" Sammie looked from me to Leighton. She was ready to burst. "I know the way."

Leighton nodded. "Certainly."

She scampered down the hall. We followed more slowly.

The family room was empty when we got there. Leighton paused. "I guess everybody's with the kittens. Come in and make yourself at home. I'm sure Hayley and Angelica will be back out in a minute."

He walked to one of the french doors and stared out over the pool and backyard. I felt awkward and realized it was because in my mind he was a suspect. Not that he could read my mind, but it was strange being in a room with someone about whom I'd had such bad thoughts.

I went to the mantel to look again at the picture of Hayley and Leighton at their wedding. The fountain *was* the same as the one in Linda's picture. So they'd been married in Atlanta. I didn't have time to think about it. I heard footsteps behind me and turned. Hayley walked through the kitchen and into the family room looking very upper-class suburban in nice slacks and a sweater set.

Leighton turned and their gazes met for a moment, then he stuck his hands in his pockets and returned to staring morosely at the pool.

Hayley looked at me. "Sammie and Angelica will be out in a minute. Sammie is just letting her kitten say good-bye to his siblings. She's sad that he has to leave his family."

That was so much like Sammie. Sometimes her sensitivity overwhelmed her.

The doorbell gonged.

"I'll go get that," Hayley said.

I turned back to the photo on the mantel, then my cell phone chirped, telling me I had a text message. I glanced at the screen. It was from Max. *Don't go to Whitmores'. I talked to Fletcher. Will explain when I can talk. And call my mother.* I squinted and read it again.

"You've figured it out, haven't you?"

I hadn't realized that Leighton had crossed the room and was standing behind me.

What had I figured out? And what was Max's message about? Had Leighton killed Philip? And had he seen my text message? I slapped my phone shut and slowly turned around. "I don't know what you mean." Not a lie. I really didn't know for sure.

"I thought we'd be safe here," he said. "Who would have thought that a drunken one-night dalliance with a stranger at a real estate convention would come back and bite me? Alcohol gives a person loose lips."

"Linda?" Her name slipped from my mouth before I could stop myself.

His head snapped toward me. "You *do* know. Your husband said you were sharp."

"I don't really know anything." I glanced at the phone in my hand. "Max is on his way." An outright lie, but it was all I could think of in the fear of the moment.

Leighton shrugged. "And if that wasn't bad enough, Philip Grenville figures out who I am. I have no idea how he did that. The company scammed his sister, not him. And him a cop. I should have moved us to Europe. Or Costa Rica."

Leighton had been part of the scam in which Mary had lost money? "Who are you?" I was trying to distract him so I could push buttons on my phone. I wished they didn't beep.

"A corporate real estate lawyer. A wanted man." He fisted his right hand and banged it into his left palm. "The people I worked for in Atlanta set up real estate deals and scammed people. They had connections, if you get my drift. When they hired me, I didn't know who they were. By the time I figured it all out, I was in too deep. They were scamming people right and left.

"They forced me to clean up the mess and point the finger at the hapless agents they'd set up to take the fall. Then they paid me to keep quiet and disappear." He paused and inhaled. "I was lucky they didn't just kill me and bury pieces of my body in some landfill."

"But what about Philip?" I asked.

"He saw me at the doctor's office one day and thought he recognized me. Only thing I could figure is he must have seen pictures of me from the investigation. He was a cop. He could have had access to that. He kept pursuing me, asking me questions. I knew if it got out, my old employers might kill me. And Hayley. I had to protect her. I married her after I changed my name, you know."

"You changed—" I was interrupted by something I saw out of the corner of my eye. I turned. So did Leighton.

"Leighton. . .honey?" Hayley had come into the room, followed closely by Clark Matthews.

Leighton frowned, then he gasped when he saw what I saw.

Clark had a gun pointed at Hayley's head.

18

What—who. . ." Leighton looked as astonished as I felt.

"Your friendly neighborhood WWPS man at your service." Clark's usual model smile had been replaced by a sneer.

Leighton took a step toward Clark. "Put your gun away and let my wife go."

"Don't move again, Mr. Leighton Whitmore," Clark said. "Of course, that's not your real name, is it?"

I began wildly pushing buttons on my cell.

"Drop that phone," Clark said to me, then jabbed the gun into Hayley's head.

I dropped it on the floor. I had one thought: Keep Sammie safe.

Leighton took a step toward Clark and Hayley.

Angelica walked into the kitchen, holding Sammie's coat in one hand and a plastic bag in the other. I heard Clark swear.

"Patricia, Samantha has been collecting things again." She finally noticed Clark. "What is going on?"

"I wondered where that bag went. Might have known the kid picked it up." Clark kept his gun pointed at Hayley's head. "Trish and Leighton, go sit on the couch."

He watched us as we obeyed. My mind was frozen. All I could think about was Sammie. What if she walked into the room?

Leighton began to clench and unclench his hands.

That brought me out of my stupor. Who was the worst bad guy here? The man next to me on the couch? Or Mr. Model Perfect, Clark? Obviously Clark had a gun, but why? And who had killed Philip?

I noticed a shadow slip into the room behind Clark. Mr. Chang Lee had finally made an appearance.

Clark paid no mind to the feline. He pointed at Angelica. "Bring me what you have in your hand."

Angelica just stood there, her mouth hanging open.

"Lady!" Clark yelled. "Do what I say, or I'm going to kill her." He shoved the gun hard into Hayley's head, and Hayley whimpered.

Leighton jumped up from the sofa, hopping across the coffee table. In one fast blur, Clark aimed his gun. The deafening shot echoed through the room. Leighton dropped to the floor next to the fireplace. A red spot bloomed near his collar on his shirt.

"No!" Hayley screamed. She raced to his side, oblivious of Clark's gun. He didn't try to stop her.

"You." Clark pointed at Angelica. "Give me what's in your hand."

She tilted her chin in the air as she walked over to him. "Whatever do you want with a bag of Tootsie Rolls and little candies?"

Clark laughed and snatched the bag from her hand. "Little candies? Lady, you live in a fantasy world. Now go sit down next to Trish."

The couch shifted slightly as Angelica sat next to me. "Where's Sammie?" I whispered.

"Where's the kid?" Clark asked at the same time.

I felt the couch shift as Angelica glanced at the doorway

to the laundry room.

Clark's sharp gaze followed hers. He smiled. "We'll take care of her in a minute."

Fear made my chest burn.

"I told her to stay with the cats for a couple of minutes while I talked to you," Angelica whispered.

"Shut up!" Clark waved the gun at us.

I begged God to keep Sammie in the laundry room. I'd lost sight of Mr. Lee, but I heard his familiar yowl.

Clark swore. "What was that?"

"Mr. Chang Lee," I said.

"Who?"

Mr. Lee strolled into the middle of the room from behind a chair, yowled again, and sat hard on his haunches, staring at Clark.

"Oh, a cat." Clark dismissed Mr. Lee with three words.

I was pretty sure he had no idea what Mr. Lee was capable of. Well, truth be told, *I* had no idea what Mr. Lee was capable of, either.

Hayley was murmuring to Leighton. She'd taken off her sweater and pressed it against his wound. It looked to me like the bullet had gone through his shoulder, but I couldn't tell for sure.

Clark turned to me. "You ask way too many questions. I should have known when you offered to take that autograph thing to my mother."

I frowned. "You should have known what?"

"I should have known you'd figure it all out. Your mother always bragged on you. And idiot Linda, all panicked because you asked her about a button. I just couldn't believe you'd be that smart. Or stupid. . .depending on how you look at it now."

That stupid. If I'd been a little smarter, I might have figured things out by now. In fact, I might have known what was actually going on

"So Linda helped you kill Philip?"

"Linda does anything I ask her to do," he said. "She's like a puppet. All I have to do is pull the strings."

Leighton hadn't killed Philip. Clark had. With Linda's help. Somehow. I thought of my earlier impression of Linda—that her eyes were like those of a stuffed animal. Maybe she really wasn't that bright.

"So what's in the bag?" I asked.

Clark glanced at the bag in his hand then stuffed it in his pocket. "Ecstasy. My bread and butter. And that cop was trying to catch me."

"But there are Tootsie Rolls in there," Angelica said.

Clark sneered at her. "The kids put the ecstasy in the Tootsie Rolls. This was for one of my customers."

Drugs. He sold drugs. I almost stopped breathing when I realized how easily Sammie could have ingested the ecstasy, thinking it was candy. I wanted to leap across the room and tear into Clark for endangering her life like that.

And that explained everything. Philip had somehow stumbled upon Clark's little business. As a narcotics cop, Philip would notice things like that. Ironically, his death had nothing to do with making amends and everything to do with his job. Like our dog, Buddy—Philip had died doing what he did best.

Now I just wanted to know how it all happened.

Angelica shifted on the couch next to me. I glanced at her. For the first time since I'd met her, I saw true fear etched across her nearly wrinkle-free brow. However, I also saw a glimpse of her haughty fury. I could relate, and it made me feel good. I reached for her hand and squeezed it. She squeezed back.

A cell phone rang in Clark's pocket. He pulled it out with his left hand and flipped it open. "Yeah, babe. Come on in. We've got some complications."

In the distance, I heard the front door open, followed by the tapping of heels coming down the wood-floored hallway.

Clark was looking around. "Where's the cat?"

I shrugged. Mr. Lee had dematerialized. The cat seemed to have almost supernatural powers to appear and reappear.

I wasn't at all surprised when Linda Faye King walked into the room. She glanced around with wide eyes. "What's going on here?"

Clark's gaze on her was disdainful, but she didn't seem to notice.

"Did you shoot someone else?" Linda asked.

Leighton groaned from the floor. "He's going to bleed to death," Hayley screamed, her eyes blazing with anger.

Clark shrugged. "He'll die no matter what. It doesn't matter."

Mr. Lee hopped up on the sofa behind me.

"I thought you said this would be easy. We'd get the money then just disappear." The pitch of Linda's voice rose. "You said no one else would have to die."

"Things happen," Clark said.

"Well, you've got the plane tickets, right?" Linda was beginning to hyperventilate. "We've got to get out of here.

Let's just tie them up and leave. No one will find us."

Clark snorted. "You are naive, babe. You have been all along."

"You cannot possibly get away with this," Angelica said.

Clark smiled. "Of course I can. I have a flight out of the country tonight. Money courtesy of Mr. Idiot Real Estate Scammer there who paid Linda to keep quiet so he wouldn't have to tell his adored wifey who he really was." Clark motioned with his head at Leighton. "Too bad he's gonna shoot all of you, set a fire, and then shoot himself."

"I knew. He told me all about it. He told me last Friday." Hayley began crying and murmuring to Leighton that it was okay.

Mr. Lee rubbed his head against mine. Not a pleasant picture, any way I looked at it. Such irony. Dying with an attack cat on one side and my mother-in-law on the other.

"What should I do now?" Linda asked Clark. "I'm not going to touch another dead body. Never again. You said I wouldn't have to."

"You touched Philip?" I asked. "You helped kill him?"

Linda shrugged. "I hated him, so it wasn't *that* bad. I had to put a receipt in his pocket. I also left that book on the counter. Our original plans didn't work out, so we pointed the finger at Abbie Grenville. Easier to do than I thought it would be."

Original plans? "Did you move his car?"

Clark smiled. "Yeah, she did." He pointed at the couch. "Linda, go sit next to Trish."

She frowned. "What?"

He aimed the gun at her. "Go sit next to Trish."

"Wait. You mean. . ." Tears filled her eyes. "But I thought—"

"You thought I loved you?" Clark laughed. "Never. I was just using you. Just like you used other people. And just like Philip used you so long ago."

Talk about what goes around comes around.

Mr. Lee jumped off the back of the couch. I heard him hit the floor with a thud. Angelica shifted next to me and took a breath as if she was going to speak. I elbowed her in the ribs to keep her quiet.

While Clark's attention was on Linda, I was trying to figure out how we could escape. The magazines on the table were thick and heavy. We could throw some, but it was risky. He might shoot one of us. The decoration book and the glass vase looked like better alternatives, but I had to have the right opportunity.

"Book," I whispered to Angelica.

Her face squished into a frown that reminded me of Charlie. I'd never noticed before the resemblance between the two. I'd never taken the time.

Linda was sobbing quietly next to me. I ignored her. She didn't deserve any sympathy. I wished I could help Hayley, who was crying over Leighton. He was bleeding profusely.

Mr. Lee appeared by my feet and butted his head against my ankles.

"I did everything for you," Linda whined at Clark. "I gave you most of the money Leighton paid me. I can't believe you're doing this. I planned it all out for you."

I turned to face her. "You planned Philip's murder?"

Clark snorted. "Hardly. That would take brains."

She pouted. Definitely lacking in the brains depart-ment. "Well, I helped." She seemed proud, and that made me want to rip out her hair by the roots. "Clark and I needed to get rid of him, because he knew about the drugs. I pretended to be nice to Philip, and then I made sure he knew Abbie would be at the church hall. See, he was all hot to make all these amends to people, including me. And he was desperate to get to Abbie alone. I'd overheard her tell your mother she'd be at the fellowship hall early that afternoon."

"I'm tired of your voice, Linda," Clark said. He was looking around the room. I imagined he was trying to figure out how best to kill us all.

She glared at him. "Well, it doesn't matter, does it?" She turned to me again like she was possessed with the need to tell me everything. "At first we were going to kill them both. I was going to lure Philip and Abbie to the back of the church. Clark was going to shoot Philip. Then we would shoot Abbie with a handgun and put her in the woods. Make it look like she shot Philip then shot herself. But then she left early in a snit. She almost ruined everything. We had to rethink fast. Killing him and making it look like Abbie had done it was *my* idea. The receipt. The book. All of it. I lured him to the back of the fellowship hall so Clark could shoot him. He had his rifle and a pistol in his truck."

She sounded so proud. I wanted to slap her. "You didn't stop to think maybe he'd already told someone else about the drugs?" I asked.

Clark and Linda both frowned. Neither one of them was too bright.

"He had no proof. And I'm tired of the talking." Clark waved the gun. "Everyone shut up."

Mr. Lee was still rubbing my ankle, but his tail was switching against Linda's leg. She kicked at him. He growled. I didn't know that cats could growl.

"Call your daughter out here," Clark ordered.

"You're no better than Philip was," Linda said, still crying. "Philip promised to leave his wife for me, but he never did. You're a traitor, too."

She kicked Mr. Lee again. His tail twitched, and he hissed and puffed up.

Clark strode over to the couch and slapped Linda. She gasped and pulled back, holding her mouth.

He pointed the gun at her head. "You're going first."

Clark took another step forward and stepped on Mr. Lee's tail. The cat yowled—the loudest I'd ever heard. I met Hayley's gaze, and one side of her mouth lifted. That's when I knew we were going to get a miracle. Mr. Lee grabbed Clark's leg with his paws and sank his front teeth into Clark's calf.

The man yelled, sounding amazingly like the cat. His gun arm flew up, and a bullet discharged into the ceiling. In one quick movement, I grabbed the vase and slammed it against his temple. As Mr. Lee bounded from the room, Clark dropped to the floor and rolled to his stomach. He was out.

"Oh, hurry," Hayley moaned. "Leighton is still bleeding, and I can't stop it, but he's alive."

I leaped from behind the table. Linda, who had been

frozen in place, suddenly came alive. She jumped up and pushed me. I stumbled over the coffee table, falling against Angelica. Suddenly I was in a race for the gun. Linda won, snatching it from the floor. Then she pointed it at me.

"No way. I can't let you get away. I'm going to finish this here and now."

Linda was not the criminal that Clark was. She didn't have the same kind of nerve. The gun in her hand was shaking, and she eyed me and Angelica nervously.

"Oh, for heaven's sake, not again," Angelica said behind me. "Will these people never stop?" I agreed with her sentiments exactly.

"Shut up," Linda said.

"Mommy?"

Angelica inhaled, breath hissing through her teeth. My stomach clenched. I felt Angelica's hand on my arm.

"Go back to the laundry room, Sammie," I said, keeping my eye on the gun in Linda's hand. It was still pointed in my direction.

"No," Linda said, gun wobbling in her hand.

"But, Mommy, the lady has a gun. It's like something Charlie—"

"Go now!" I yelled.

"Don't go." Since the gun in Linda's hand still pointed at me, I knew she wouldn't shoot Sammie, but I was poised to launch myself between my daughter and a gunshot.

I heard Sammie's feet patter down the hallway.

Linda's eyes wavered between me and the hall where Sammie had disappeared. "Call her back out here."

I said nothing. I wouldn't. I would never call Sammie back into the room without a fight. I hadn't given up hope that we would find a way out of this.

Clark groaned. Linda's eyes widened with fear. If he woke up, we were all in trouble. I exchanged glances with Angelica, and she narrowed her eyes and gave me a slight smile. That's when I knew our second miracle was coming.

She gasped suddenly and pointed at the doorway behind Linda. "Oh no—watch out! Here comes that cat! He's vicious."

The cat wasn't even in sight, but the distraction was exactly what we needed. Linda turned, long enough for me to grab a magazine, lunge at her, and slap her hand away from us. The gun clattered to the floor.

Angelica hopped to her feet, snatched up the decorating book, and walloped Linda across the head with it. That stunned her and allowed me to push her into a chair and grab the gun.

Hayley reached over and snatched my cell phone from the floor where I'd dropped it. "I'm calling 911."

"Good," I said. I stared at my mother-in-law with amazement. "Wow. Way to go, Angelica." I had never been prouder of anyone in my life.

For the first time since I'd met her, we shared grins. I hadn't known she *could* grin.

"The curtain ties will do well to contain those two, don't you think?" she asked as she glided over to the windows.

"Yes, I believe they will."

Hayley's voice was hysterical on the phone. Linda was crying and babbling as we tied her up. She didn't fight us. She was a wimp. Too bad. I was ready to take someone on.

Clark, on the other hand, was not a wimp. And he probably lifted weights to keep his model shape. He began to come to as Angelica finished wrapping maroon ties around his wrists. As soon as he figured out what was going on, he swore and tried to get up on his knees. I used my foot to shove him off balance, then I sat hard on his legs while Angelica tied his feet. When she was done, I bounced for good measure, making Clark groan. Not hard for me to do. I kept thinking what would have happened if Sammie had eaten some of the ecstasy. I was furious.

"Please go take care of Sammie," I said to Angelica.

But she didn't have to. Sammie walked into the room holding a phone.

"I called the police," she said proudly. "They're here."

I heard banging at the front door. Then I heard a voice I thought I'd never be glad to hear.

"State police!" Detective Reid bellowed down the hall. "Put your weapons down."

19

Later that evening, I was perched on a chair in my mother's kitchen holding Sammie, who cuddled her kitten in her lap. Abbie was sitting across the table from me. She still had circles under her eyes, but the tension that had lined her face for days was gone. Ma had just hung up the phone and dropped into a chair at the end of the table. Eric and Daddy leaned against the counter. A little black-and-white border collie puppy scampered on the floor between their legs.

"Well, Trish, you helped nail a killer," Ma said, glancing at Eric.

He winked at me.

"Did you know that Nick Fletcher and I were working together?" I asked him.

He nodded. "I did. And I have to say, I was relieved. He was feeding information to someone at the state police. They were already closing in on Clark. And Leighton."

"So Detective Reid isn't all bad?" I asked the question reluctantly.

Eric shook his head. "Personality challenged and stubborn. Perhaps too eager at first to believe that Abbie did it. But she did look into the other information when she got the information. I can't fault her for that."

"So the cops were already onto Clark, weren't they?" I asked. "He was an idiot to think he could get away."

He nodded. "Clark would have been arrested shortly."

I bit my lip as I thought. "Do you think that's what

Philip was calling you about the day he was murdered? Had he learned what Clark was doing?"

"I think so," Eric said. "I think he had suspicions, anyway."

"I think Clark is a sociopath," I said. "And he certainly had his mother fooled." I rummaged through my purse and pulled out my steno pad and a pen. "I've dubbed him the Kitty Litter Killer for the litter next to Philip's body."

I wrote "Kitty Litter Killer" across the cardboard front of the notebook and stared at it. This would be my last mystery. No more.

I glanced across the table and met Abbie's gaze. My best friend.

"So what about the kitty litter?" Abbie asked. "How did it get next to Philip's body?"

"From Clark's shoes, right?" I glanced at Eric.

"That's what Detective Reid thinks," he said.

"When the police roared into the Whitmores', Linda started babbling. One of the things she said was that Clark used the containers or packages of things he was delivering to hide drugs sometimes. Twice he used bags of kitty litter destined for the Adlers' store. One of those times was right before he killed Philip.

"They happened to be at the Gas 'n' Go at the same time. Clark panicked and shoved his handgun into a bag of litter. The litter fell all over the truck, and he stepped in it." I looked at Abbie. "That was the gun they were going to use to make it look like you killed yourself after you shot Philip."

"Well, all's well that ends well," Ma said, patting Abbie's hand.

Abbie smiled at me, and for the first time in almost a week, her eyes smiled, too. "Thank you. You've saved my wedding day."

"It wasn't all me," I said.

We touched index fingers.

Sammie wiggled in my lap.

"I'm so proud of you, honey," I whispered in her ear.

"I did what Charlie would have done," she said. "Mommy, you're squeezing me too tight—I can hardly breathe. Can I go watch TV?"

"Sure." I didn't want to let her go, but I did.

"I thought for sure Henry had done it," Ma said. "Their granddaughter is Philip's daughter, right?"

Eric nodded. "And Henry gave Philip the black eye at the store that Sunday afternoon. Philip wanted to see his daughter. Peggy, the Adlers' daughter, was seventeen when Philip got her pregnant. The Adlers agreed not to report him to the authorities if he signed an agreement giving away his parental rights. That was the deal. Henry was furious when Philip came back. But he wanted to see his daughter before he died."

"It's like a soap opera," Ma said.

Daddy nodded. "That's the truth."

"Well, there might be a happy ending," Abbie said. "The Adlers have contacted June. They're still having trouble with this, but they have promised that at some point, June will meet her granddaughter. June says she's going to be patient."

"Are you okay about it all?" I asked her.

Abbie and Eric exchanged a glance, then she looked at me. "It's hard. Especially when I look back and realize how all the choices I made keep reverberating through the years." She smiled, but her expression held an edge of sadness. "It will take me awhile to take it all in, I think, but I get to start over." Suddenly she grinned. "And I have a fine man to start over with."

She stood and walked over to Eric. He wrapped his arm around her shoulders.

Max strolled into the room and kissed my forehead.

"Chris is finally asleep."

"Good."

"Honey, I'm sorry," he said. "I should have paid attention to your suspicions about Leighton. This afternoon never would have happened. You wouldn't have even been there to confront Clark. Nick Fletcher called me to ask a few more questions about what I knew about Leighton Whitmore. He explained why he was asking. That's why I warned you not to go over there. And when I realized you and Mom and Sammie were already at the Whitmores', I called Nick back. They were already on their way over there when Sammie called them."

I grasped his hand, and he pulled me to my feet. "Well, if it hadn't worked out the way it did, we might never have known exactly what Clark and Linda had planned. That they were going to kill Leighton and Hayley then burn down the house. Make it look like a murder-suicide. As if Leighton just got tired of running from his past."

"I certainly hope Whitmore is going to jail," Ma said.

Eric shook his head. "I'm not sure. He may testify against his former employers and then go into witness protection."

I heard the sound of the back door opening. Angelica

and Andrew walked in from the mudroom. I'd never been so surprised to see anyone in my life.

Ma, bless her heart, hurried across the room and greeted them as if they dropped by every day.

"Did you know they were coming?" I asked Max.

He nodded, and humor sparkled in his eyes.

After Angelica said hello to my mother, she crossed the room and pulled me into a hug. The hush that fell over the kitchen told me everyone else was as shocked as I was. If she hadn't had her arms around me, I would have fallen to the floor.

She stepped back, hands still on my arms. "You made me so proud today."

"Thank you," I said.

Apparently no one expected this from her, me included. I was at a loss for words.

Daddy cleared his throat. "Hey, how about the whole story. I wanna know what happened."

Angelica and I took turns telling everyone about the chilling scene at the Whitmores'.

"So how did Linda get the money to run away with Clark?" my mother asked.

"She recognized Leighton when he moved here and approached him," I said. "She'd met him at a real estate convention in Atlanta and had a one-night fling. In his drunken state, he told her things he didn't even remember telling her." I paused. "She's someone who takes advantage of a situation when it arises."

"Gail was right, you know," Ma said. "I'll never forgive myself."

I smiled at her then continued my story. "Linda

started dating Clark. And after Philip caught on to Clark's dealings, she told Clark she had a way to get money to help them move to a safe place. Being what he was, he decided to take her up on that. Leighton was frightened of his former employers and wanted to protect Hayley. He offered Linda a million dollars to leave him alone."

"What about Leighton and Philip?" Ma asked.

I glanced at Eric.

"I can only speculate at this point," he said. He explained about Mary losing money in a real estate deal. "I think Philip figured out who Leighton was and wanted to talk to him. That scared Leighton, which was why he began making plans to move."

"He had me and Angelica snowed," Max's father said. "His resumé was faked. The folks he had worked for were organized. They knew if Leighton went to jail that he'd blow the whistle on the organization, so they arranged to protect him and give him a new identity. He thought they'd be safe in a small town like this. Hayley had no idea."

"She's the one I feel sorriest for." I glanced at Angelica. "She did nothing wrong except love her husband."

"It's all about choices," Abbie said.

The back door opened again. Gail walked into the kitchen.

"My lands. Looks like a used-car lot out there." Ma's longtime employee smiled, looking like the Gail I used to know. She rubbed her hands together to warm them. She stared at me then at Eric. "You should hire Trish, you know. You need her to help you solve crimes and keep this town safe." She glanced at Ma and they nodded.

"I agree," Ma said.

I smiled. The town was safe once again. Gossip central was back in business. Ma and Gail were friends again.

"Well, we hope Tommy inherited Trish's good sense by osmosis," Angelica said. "If he handles a law enforcement job the way she handled the situation today, he'll do fine."

I glanced at her to make sure she wasn't being sarcastic. She was smiling at me—really smiling. The Lord had used a bad situation to bring about a miracle. I was sure things wouldn't be perfect, but we had a good start. And a chance at a real relationship.

Epilogue

I stood at the front of the church in my green dress, holding a bouquet of ivy, a red rose, and a white rose with red tints. Abbie said they were like me and her. I was the red rose. All heat and outright emotion. She was the white rose with hidden passions.

White Christmas lights, ivy, and evergreen adorned the pews and the platforms.

I glanced over the crowd of people, recognizing so many faces, thankful they had come out to help two special people celebrate their second chance at love. My mother clutched a tissue. On her right side sat Gail. On her left, Sammie and Charlie sat remarkably still. I smiled when I realized I no longer had to worry that Sammie might slip items in her pockets during the reception. She'd stopped doing that as soon as she brought the kitten home.

Max sat next to Charlie. I caught his eye. He smiled, a slow and very personal smile. I felt it down to my toes.

Eric stood tall and handsome in a black tux. Next to him stood Nick Fletcher and Tommy.

The sanctuary doors opened. Sherry walked down the aisle, and the handkerchief hem of her green dress whirled around her ankles. She held a bouquet of ivy and three roses that represented her new family—Eric, Abbie, and Sherry.

When Sherry reached the front of the church, she

handed me her bouquet then walked over to Eric and gave him a big hug and kiss—the unrehearsed, impulsive moment perfect. He pulled her tight and whispered something in her ear. Then she walked over to join me with a smile.

The music stopped. We waited for my very best friend to come through the doors on the arm of my father. I slid my gaze to Eric watching the door at the back of the church with a boyish eagerness that belied his age. Nick met my gaze and winked.

When the "Wedding March" began, Abbie appeared in her silky ivory dress with rich lace on the sleeves. Slowly she made her way down the aisle on my grinning father's arm.

When Abbie reached the front, Daddy placed her hand in Eric's. Abbie looked over at me and extended her index finger. I returned the gesture as a precious reminder of a friendship that would never end.

As Eric and Abbie turned to the pastor, I remembered a sermon I'd heard once about heaven. Only people enter into eternity, not possessions or money. I was glad Philip had learned that before he died.

Love was all about choices. I wished Linda had understood that before she hooked up with Clark. True love isn't demanding or grasping. True love is unselfish and gives. A healthy love—God's love—always hopes for the best, and it sometimes means sacrificing for another.

And that's what we were celebrating today with Abbie and Eric. True love that stands the test of time and lasts forever.

Candice Speare lives in Maryland surrounded by cornfields and cattle. She spends most days in her second-story office in the company of Winston, the African Gray Parrot. Candice is the author of two published books, *Murder in the Milk Case* and *Band Room Bash*, the first two books in the Trish Cunningham series. Besides plotting fictional murder and mayhem, she is an amateur photographer and fiddles with digital images. She also dabbles in Web site design. When she has the time, she likes to garden, scrapbook, sew, and play the piano—especially worship music. She loves to collect recipes and on occasion has even been known to remove one from the file drawer and make it. Rumors of her eccentricities are true. Please visit her Web site at www.candicemillerspeare.com, where you can read her blog and find out more information about contests for her readers, as well as upcoming events and new releases.

You may correspond with this author by writing:
Candice Speare
Author Relations
PO Box 721
Uhrichsville, OH 44683

A Letter to Our Readers

Dear Reader:
In order to help us satisfy your quest for more great mystery stories, we would appreciate it if you would take a few minutes to respond to the following questions. We welcome your comments and read each form and letter we receive. When completed, please return to:

Fiction Editor
Heartsong Presents—MYSTERIES!
PO Box 721
Uhrichsville, Ohio 44683

Did you enjoy reading *Kitty Litter Killer* by Candice Speare?

Very much! I would like to see more books like this! The one thing I particularly enjoyed about this story was:

_____
_____
_____

Moderately. I would have enjoyed it more if:

_____
_____
_____

Are you a member of the HP—MYSTERIES! Book Club?
Yes   No

If no, where did you purchase this book?

_____

Please rate the following elements using a scale of 1 (poor) to 10 (superior):

___ Main character/sleuth   ___ Romance elements

___ Inspirational theme   ___ Secondary characters

___ Setting   ___ Mystery plot

How would you rate the cover design on a scale of 1 (poor) to 5 (superior)? _____

What themes/settings would you like to see in future **Heartsong Presents—MYSTERIES!** selections? _____

_____

_____

_____

Please check your age range:
- ○ Under 18   ○ 18–24
- ○ 25–34   ○ 35–45
- ○ 46–55   ○ Over 55

Name: _____

Occupation: _____

Address: _____

E-mail address: _____